BEHIND THE
BEDROOM
WALL

BEHIND THE BEDROOM WALL

by Laura E. Williams

Illustrations by A. Nancy Goldstein

SCHOLASTIC INC.

New York Toronto London Auckland Sydney
Mexico City New Delhi Hong Kong Buenos Aires

ISBN-13: 978-0-590-21415-5
ISBN-10: 0-590-21415-2

12 11 10 9 8 7 6 5 4 3 2 1   6 7 8 9 10 11/0

Printed in the U.S.A.   40

This edition printing, September 2006

This book is dedicated to my parents,
Sally Williams and Bill Fuller,
who allowed me to make my own choices.
And to children everywhere, who know how hard
those choices are to make.

Thanks go to the many people who gave their time, advice,
and knowledge in the shaping of this book.

Special thanks go to the people at Milkweed Editions
for all they've done, and to Leopold and Maria Sans
for their memories.

Thanks also to my agent, Edy Selman, who is lavish with
her praise and honest with her criticism.

Behind the Bedroom Wall

Chapter One

"Jew-lover!" spat the tall, blond Gestapo officer, pushing Herr Haase toward the car. Herr Haase, wearing no jacket or shoes against the February cold, slipped on a patch of ice and fell.

Frau Haase stood in the open doorway of her house. Her two children clutched her skirt, watching their father with wide, tear-filled eyes.

"Get up, Jew-lover!" said a second officer, his dark leather boots glinting in the fading evening light. He kicked the fallen man. "Get up or I'll shoot you now just to get it over with," he threatened.

Herr Haase slowly rose to his knees, one arm clamped to his side where he had been kicked. On the icy snow where his head had rested, a patch of red stained the whiteness.

"Faster!" the first officer commanded. He nudged Herr Haase with his boot so that the prisoner faltered again before he finally struggled to his feet.

Three girls stood on the opposite side of the road, watching, their blue and white *Jungmädel* uniforms hidden under their heavy woolen coats.

"Isn't Hans handsome?" Rita asked proudly, as her tall, blond brother viciously kicked Herr Haase again.

"I think it's just awful," Eva whispered, her voice quivering slightly. "Why are they beating poor Herr Haase? What's he done wrong?"

Korinna shifted her bulky book bag from one frozen hand to the other. "They're calling him a Jew-lover."

"Who'd want to hide a stinking Jew? Besides, he'd be dead already if he'd been hiding a Jew," Rita said. "I heard Hans tell Papa they're supposed to shoot first and ask questions later. Herr Haase must have been seen talking to a Jew."

"How can it be so terrible just to be talking to a Jew?" Eva asked, shaking her head, her short, dirty blond hair swinging against her cheeks.

Rita looked at her sideways, her eyes narrowing slightly. "You don't see anything wrong with it?" she asked, forgetting to keep her voice down. "Jews are the enemy! They are the root of all our problems. Without them Germany will be strong!"

Korinna nodded absently in agreement, even as she winced as one of the officers shoved Herr Haase toward the car.

Eva kicked at a mound of snow. "I don't think—"

"My brother wouldn't arrest just anyone," Rita interrupted, flipping her long, blond braid over her shoulder like a whip. "Herr Haase is a traitor to Germany. He's been fooling everyone into thinking he's a nice man by giving extra meat from his butcher shop to the poor people, but that was just a cover-up. He's a traitor, or why would they arrest him?"

She pointed across the street as though to prove her point. The Gestapo officers pushed Herr Haase into the back of the car.

Korinna suddenly remembered the hard candies the butcher had always given her when she used to visit his shop with her mother before the war had started. Pity for him welled up in her. Immediately she squashed it. He must be an enemy for Hans to be arresting him, she told herself firmly. It would be un-German of her to pity a traitor.

The car roared off. Without a word, Eva turned from her two comrades and fled down the street through the thickening gloom.

Rita shook her head. "Eva's stupid. One day, someone is going to turn her in for being un-German. She almost sounds like a Jew-lover herself."

"Leave her alone," Korinna said to her best friend. "You know how Eva is. She cries when someone kills a wasp. She'll get over this."

Rita shrugged. "She's a baby. When the Führer makes Germany strong again, and we can all hold up our heads, she won't feel so sorry for those Jew-lovers."

Korinna stomped her feet to warm them up. "You're right, but I'm freezing. Let's go."

Rita smiled and took Korinna's arm. For a moment, they walked quietly arm in arm. Then Rita said, "Wasn't our meeting fun today?"

Korinna laughed. "You looked so funny with all that flour in your hair."

Rita grinned. "Don't worry, I'll get Ute back at our next meeting. I wonder how she'll look with flour in *her* hair, and all over her uniform, too!"

"You wouldn't!" Korinna said with a gasp.

Rita just looked at her and laughed.

"Poor Ute," Korinna moaned. "The poor girl didn't know what she was starting."

Still laughing, Rita said, "Did you ask your mother if you could come over for dinner?"

Korinna nodded. "But she said you should come over to our house instead. Sometime this week."

Rita squeezed her arm. "I'd like that. Your mother is the best cook around."

When they came to the corner where they parted, they simply waved at each other. Best friends didn't need to say anything, Korinna thought as she walked home. And Rita had been her best friend for two years now, ever since they had both turned eleven and discovered that their birthdays were in the same week.

Rita was like the sister she'd always wanted. They shared all their secrets and dreams. They shared everything. But, of course, that's what best friends were for.

———————

"Mother, I'm home!" Korinna called as she stepped into the cozy warmth of her house. She put down her heavy book bag and immediately pulled off her winter boots and coat. Her fingers and toes started to tingle painfully as they warmed up. It felt as though someone were stabbing her with millions of needles.

Frau Rehme came through the kitchen door. "Hello, *Liebling*." She kissed her daughter's cheek. "Brrrr. You feel like an icicle." She smiled and took Korinna's hands between her own and rubbed them vigorously back and forth. "How was school?"

Korinna shrugged. "The same. We received new history books today, though."

"Oh, really? What was wrong with the old ones?"

"We had to paste together too many pages because our teacher told us those pages were no longer accurate. Things are changing so quickly that we needed an updated book."

Her mother squeezed Korinna's chilly hands. "But history doesn't change," she said softly. "Just people's perception of it."

"What did you say?"

Frau Rehme shook her head. "Nothing, dear. Nothing important."

Korinna shrugged and pulled her hands free. "It must be Rita yelling in my ear all the time. It's making me deaf. Anyway, our new books have pages and pages about our Führer and all he's doing for Germany. He's making jobs for people. He has such exciting plans for us all. Hitler is the most wonderful man, Mother. Don't you think so?"

Frau Rehme looked at the framed picture of Adolf Hitler hanging above the couch. "Yes, he's a wonderful man," she said slowly.

Korinna hugged her. "Don't worry, Mother, the Führer says it's only a matter of weeks, months at the most, before Germany will be great again and we win the war."

Frau Rehme sighed and looked as if she were about to say something, but instead she turned and walked back into the kitchen. Korinna followed her.

"Where's Papa?"

"He's correcting school papers upstairs. Call him for supper, please."

Korinna walked halfway up the narrow stairs to the second floor of the house where the two bedrooms were. She shivered in the cold stairway. "Papa," she called. "Time to eat!" She waited until she heard the scrape of his chair being pushed back, then she hurried downstairs to the warmth of the kitchen.

"The butcher was arrested tonight," Korinna said, once they were sitting down to eat.

"Herr Haase?" her mother asked sharply, glancing at her husband.

Korinna nodded. "Hans Damerau was one of the officers. Rita and Eva and I saw the whole thing. They called Herr Haase a Jew-lover."

"Oh, my God!" Frau Rehme exclaimed, nearly dropping her fork. "A Jew-lover! Poor Frau Haase. What will she do with those little children? She'll have to work extra long hours to keep food on the table. No one will help her now that her husband's been arrested. It will be too dangerous."

"Someone will help her," comforted Korinna's father. "Herr Haase helped many people. No one will forget it that quickly."

Korinna looked up from her plate, her eyes wide with surprise. "But he's a Jew-lover. Why would anyone dare to help a traitor or his family?"

"First of all, we don't know for sure Herr Haase is, in fact, a so called 'Jew-lover,' and secondly, it's none of our business," Herr Rehme said firmly. "And I don't want you standing around watching people get arrested. It's dangerous."

Korinna shrugged. She didn't see anything dangerous about watching an arrest. She didn't see many of them because they usually happened late at night when she was asleep, but she was glad to see traitors to Germany get arrested.

She shifted in her chair, trying not to picture the blood on Herr Haase's head, or the wide, sad eyes of his children. If he were a traitor to Germany, then it was right he should be taken away. It was all for the good of the Fatherland.

While her parents ate in silence, Korinna played with a piece of bread on her plate.

"Why aren't you eating?" her mother asked, eyeing Korinna's full plate.

"I'm not really hungry," she said, intently studying the tines of her fork.

Korinna's father raised his bushy, red eyebrows. "Not hungry? Hundreds of poor people would do anything for what you have on your plate, and you say you're not hungry?"

Korinna didn't look up. "After our hike, we—we made sweet buns."

"Sweet buns? For what?"

"Just to eat, I guess. Anyway, they weren't very sweet because we didn't have enough sugar. Just a couple of pinches."

"Don't you do anything worthwhile at those *Jungmädel* meetings?" her father growled.

Korinna brightened. "Oh yes, we help the poor and babysit for people. And today we got bundles of new pamphlets to pass out. They're very nice. They even have the Führer's picture on the front. Would you like to see them?"

Her father put down his fork with a loud clang. "No!"

Her mother stood to clear the table. "Maybe later. Right now your father is tired. It's been a long day at school for him, too."

Herr Rehme pushed himself away from the table and took out a pipe from his pocket. "Every day gets longer," he said, sighing. "Longer and longer."

Korinna looked at her father. He looked tired and so did her mother. "Maybe I shouldn't be in the *Jungmädel*. Especially now that we're often meeting more than once a week."

"What?" her mother said, her hand poised above the pile of dirty dishes.

"Maybe I should come home after school and help you. I can help you clean and cook, and in the summer I can work in the garden."

Herr Rehme drew on his pipe to light it. "No, you'll go to the meetings just the way you have been."

"But Mother looks tired," Korinna insisted. "I want to help her."

"You'll help her by going to the meetings, Korinna." Her father removed the smoking pipe from his mouth and used the stem as a pointer for emphasis. "It would be un-German of you not to be a member of *Jungmädel*. You would get into trouble for quitting."

Korinna smiled. "Oh no, Papa, the leaders at the *Jungmädel* are very nice. They wouldn't think I'm un-German just for wanting to stay home to help Mother."

Korinna's parents glanced at each other.

Her mother plunged the dishes into the steaming water. "That's very thoughtful of you, dear, but we don't want you to give up your meetings. We know you enjoy them. You just go and have fun."

"Are you sure?"

"Yes," her father said firmly, blowing out a big puff of fragrant smoke. Then he smiled. "I have a surprise for you."

Korinna clapped her hands together. "Really? What is it?"

Korinna's father checked his pockets as if he were looking for something. "Now where did I put it? Helga, do you know where I put it?"

His wife smiled, but shook her head.

He finally knocked his broad knuckles on his forehead. "Oh, I remember, next to my boots."

Korinna frowned. "In the hall, Papa?"

"Go look, I tell you. Quickly!"

Korinna got up from the table and walked to the front hall where she had left her book bag. Next to her father's large boots sat a box she hadn't noticed before. Someone had punched holes in the top. Korinna held her breath and slowly lifted the lid. Inside, a small bundle of fur trembled in one corner. Korinna gently lifted the little black and white kitten out of the box and, hugging it close, walked back into the kitchen.

"Oh, Papa," she said breathlessly, "he's beautiful! Look at the little white nose! Thank you so much! I'll take good care of him, I promise."

"I think he's a she, but you're welcome. She comes from a long line of mice killers."

"Don't tease her, Bernd," Korinna's mother chided.

Korinna blushed. "I heard the mice, Papa. I swear it. They live behind my bedroom wall."

"I know, I'm just teasing you. I put a mousetrap up there for them. Did you hear any mice last night?"

"No, not last night."

Her father nodded with approval. "Good. The traps must have scared the little rodents away. Anyway, now if they come back you have a mouse-catcher."

"Thank you," Korinna said, touching her nose to the kitten's. "What shall I call her?"

Herr Rehme shrugged. "That's your decision, Korinna. I trust you'll make the right choice."

Korinna glanced over at her father, looking for the teasing glint in his eyes, but instead he looked quite serious. She wouldn't have thought that naming a cat would be such a serious event, but then, she'd never had a cat before.

"Don't worry, Papa," she said, hoping she sounded solemn enough for this occasion. "You can trust me to make the right choice."

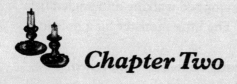

Chapter Two

By morning, Korinna still hadn't chosen a name for her new kitten. The black and white "mouse-catcher" raced around in crazy circles and made flying leaps at Korinna's stockinged legs as she dressed.

After a cold breakfast of rye bread spread with a thin layer of jam, Korinna left her kitten purring next to the coal stove in the kitchen.

"I'm leaving, Mother," Korinna called from the front hall, shouldering her book bag.

Frau Rehme came from the kitchen, wiping her hands on a towel and hugged her daughter. "Come home right after school today. Aunt Hendrikia is coming over for dinner."

"I won't forget," Korinna promised as she slipped out into the cold morning air. She pulled the door shut behind her.

Korinna stomped her feet to keep warm as Rita and Eva crunched over to her through the snow.

"*Heil Hitler,*" Rita called.

Korinna returned the greeting. "*Heil Hitler.* Guess what?" she added as she joined her friends, and they continued on toward school. "Papa gave me a kitten to catch the mice I heard. She's the cutest little thing. And look." Korinna stopped walking and angled her calf to show them. "The little monster bit a hole in my stocking!"

"What does the kitty look like?" Eva asked.

"She's black and white and so fuzzy. Maybe you can help me name her."

Eva sighed. "I wish I could have a kitty. But, of course, I don't have any mice in my walls."

Korinna shuddered. "I hope the traps really did scare the mice away. What if I ever saw a mouse race across my floor? I'm scared of them."

Giggling, Eva said, "I know what I'd do—I'd scream."

Korinna nodded. "And I'd—"

Rita made an impatient sound in the back of her throat. "Wait until you hear this," she interrupted, slicing her hand through the air for emphasis. "Hans stopped by last night. Guess why Herr Haase was taken away."

"Why?" Korinna asked flatly.

"He was involved in a secret organization that helps Jews! He's being taken to the work camp, but first they're going to try to find out who else is in the organization."

Korinna shrugged. "Maybe he'll never say who else was in the organization."

"My brother says they have methods for extracting secrets out of prisoners."

Eva's eyes widened. "He told you all this?"

Rita shook her head. "I heard him talking to Papa in the kitchen. They didn't know I was listening."

"What kind of methods?" Korinna couldn't help asking.

"Secret methods," Rita said, her voice a loud whisper. "Hans isn't even allowed to tell his own father.

"And look at this," she continued, taking a small notebook out of the pocket in her coat.

Korinna and Eva looked at what Rita had scratched into the book in her messy scrawl.

"Fräulein Demmer made a face at the Führer's picture," Korinna read out loud. "She says it's a sin what's happening to the Jews. When she sees me she looks guilty and doesn't say anything more for the rest of the night." Korinna stopped reading suddenly. "Fräulein Demmer? You mean Elsa Demmer?"

Rita nodded smugly.

"But, Rita, Elsa's your cousin! You're going to turn in your cousin?" Eva exclaimed.

Rita's face turned red. "She's an enemy of Germany, isn't she? She shouldn't be so sympathetic to the enemy, and if she weren't so guilty, why did she avoid me for the rest of the night? She knows she's wrong!"

"But still, Rita, family . . ." Eva started walking again.

Korinna put a hand on Eva's shoulder. "Remember, even family members can turn against the new Germany."

Rita snapped the small notebook shut. "They said to watch *everyone*."

Korinna nodded. She had a little black notebook just like Rita's. "Hurry up," she said. "We'll be late." They ran the last few hundred meters to the school and quickly made their way to their classroom.

Korinna and Eva were deskmates. Rita sat across the room. History was their favorite subject, especially with all the exciting events that were currently taking place. Someday, Korinna knew, every student in the world, every person in the world, in fact, would know the name Adolf Hitler. Everyone would honor and love him as she did, and everyone would say what wonderful things he'd done for Germany, the strongest and greatest power in the world. Korinna smiled, opening her new history book.

"Heil Hitler!"

Korinna looked up, startled.

"I am Herr Richt, your new history teacher. Fräulein Meiser will no longer be here. Today we are going to study . . ."

Korinna didn't hear the rest of Herr Richt's comments. Where was Fräulein Meiser? Beautiful Fräulein Meiser with her long blond braid she wore wound up on her head like an upside-down basket—

what had happened to her? Korinna tried to swallow past the lump in her throat. Her eyes slid sideways to Eva. Eva stared forward, but her eyes glimmered with tears, and her hands were clasped tightly in front of her.

Korinna looked down at the desk. What was it Fräulein Meiser had said last week? She had been instructing the class as to which pages they should paste together in their history books when, in the middle of it all, she had suddenly sighed and looked at the ceiling. "When will all this stop?" she had asked the ceiling. "When?" Then she had shaken her head and continued reading off the list of forbidden pages.

Korinna now remembered she had found it disturbing enough to mark it down in her small notebook.

And, that day after school, she had read her notes to her *Jungmädel* leaders. She had tried to gloss over this little bit of information about her history teacher, not thinking that it was very important in retrospect. But her leaders had seemed particularly interested in what Fräulein Meiser had said during class that morning.

Now, Korinna wondered if she had had something to do with Fräulein Meiser's disappearance from school. Surely what her teacher had said in class wasn't enough to send her away. Or was it?

Korinna tried to concentrate on the lesson, but Herr Richt had a voice that crept along like a slug in her mother's garden.

Finally, when the history lesson was over, Korinna followed Eva out of the room for break. "Eva," she called.

Eva stopped and turned.

"Do you know why Fräulein Meiser isn't going to teach anymore?"

Eva shook her head. "Someone probably reported her as being un-German," she said bitterly.

Korinna pulled a loose thread on her sweater. "She wouldn't be arrested just for saying something that sounded disloyal, would she?"

"Who knows these days? One can never be too careful. Poor Fräulein Meiser." She shook her head and started walking down the hall.

Korinna hurried and walked along beside Eva. "I know you feel bad about what we saw yesterday. You know, with Herr Haase. But you should watch what you say. Rita thinks you're sounding un-German."

Eva stopped walking and turned to Korinna. Her lips trembled, and tears threatened to tip over her lower lashes. "You know," Eva said slowly, "I can't help the way I feel about things. I want a strong and rich Fatherland just like my comrades. But sometimes I honestly wonder if it's worth it."

"Eva!" Korinna lowered her voice, quickly looking around, but no one was paying them any attention. "You mustn't say things like that! If anyone heard you talking like that you'd be turned in to our *Jungmädel* leaders."

"You're the only one who heard me, Korinna. Are you going to turn me in?"

Korinna stared at her friend, her comrade, her fellow *Jungmädel* member. But part of being a loyal German was turning in traitors.

"I'm going back to class," Korinna said abruptly. She turned and walked away from Eva, but she could feel Eva's eyes staring after her.

Chapter Three

When Korinna got home after school, she didn't call out to her mother, whom she heard talking to Aunt Hendrikia in the other room. First she wanted to find her kitten.

Quietly, she took off her boots and hung up her coat in the small front hall. Her father wasn't home yet. She could tell because his big boots weren't in their usual place under the small square mirror hanging on the wall.

Korinna slipped past the front room where her mother and aunt sat talking and stepped silently up the narrow stairs to her bedroom. In her room, she deposited her book bag neatly on the floor next to her *Schrank*. She picked up a ribbon off the floor. How did that get there? she wondered.

She bent down and looked under her bed for her kitten. She also looked behind her chair and under her small desk.

Still stepping softly, Korinna moved next door into her parents' room. Again she looked under the bed and in various other possible hideaways she thought a kitten might fit into.

"Here kitty, kitty," she called softly. "Here kitty, kitty." Nothing. No scratching, no answering meow.

With a sigh, Korinna resigned herself to the fact that her kitten must be downstairs in the kitchen or in the front room with her mother. She returned to her room and lay down on her soft feather bed and closed her eyes for just a minute. The subdued murmuring floating up from downstairs soothed her.

———————

"Korinna!"

Korinna's eyes flew open. The afternoon glow had vanished from her room, leaving an eerie shroud of darkness in its place.

"Korinna," her mother said again. "Are you ill?" She walked over and placed a hand on her daughter's forehead. "Why didn't you come in and see Auntie? Now she's left."

Korinna sat up. "Sorry, Mother. I was going to come down, but I must have fallen asleep. Is Aunt Hendrikia angry?"

"I think her feelings were hurt more than anything."

"Is that why she left so early? I thought she was staying for dinner."

"She did, Korinna. She's eaten and gone," Frau Rehme said, tucking a loose strand of Korinna's reddish gold hair behind her ear.

Korinna gasped. "What time is it?"

"Nearly five."

"Why didn't you wake me to eat?" Korinna asked.

"I let you sleep because I thought you might be ill."

"I was just tired. Today was a long day," Korinna said. Her stomach rumbled. "Is there any food left?" she asked hopefully.

Frau Rehme smiled. "There's a plate fixed for you downstairs. Go now while it's still hot."

Korinna hugged her mother and trotted downstairs to the kitchen. The bright, warm kitchen smelled of the sweet scent of sugar buns and cake—two extra special treats reserved for days when they had guests, especially now that the price of sugar and shortening was so high and nearly impossible to get, thanks to the war. But of course it was worth it, she reminded herself hastily. As her *Jungmädel* leaders always said, no sacrifice for the Fatherland was too great.

Sitting down, she glanced around the small room for her tiny black and white kitten, but she didn't see her. Korinna felt a twinge of disappointment that her kitten hadn't come scrambling for her the minute she'd walked in the door, and now it even seemed to be hiding on purpose.

Korinna quickly finished eating and walked into the front room, the only other room they had

25

downstairs. It was empty. Not even her father filled his overstuffed chair as he did every night after supper, blowing smoke rings at imaginary targets.

Checking once more behind the long sofa, Korinna finally gave up her search for her kitten and went back upstairs.

"Mother," Korinna called, walking into her parents' bedroom. The room was empty. Puzzled, she turned around and walked into her own room. Her mother stood in the middle of the floor, gently stroking the head of her kitten.

"Where did you find her?" Korinna exclaimed, taking the kitten from her mother's hands.

"She was under your bed."

"But I checked under the bed."

"Maybe she slipped in while you were eating," her mother suggested.

"Maybe." She rubbed the silken head. "Where's Papa?" she asked, changing the subject.

"He's at a school meeting."

Korinna raised her eyebrows. "This late?"

Frau Rehme reached over and patted the kitten's tiny head. "He came home and left again. You slept through it."

"When will he be home?"

"Soon. Seven at the latest."

"What time is it now?"

Frau Rehme checked her watch. "Twenty until six."

"Oh no!" Korinna exclaimed, heading toward the door.

"What's wrong?"

Korinna dashed down the stairs, her kitten still clutched in her arms. "The Führer's speaking on the radio!"

As her mother followed her down, Korinna turned on the old radio to the official station. Already Adolf Hitler's voice was traveling over the radio waves with a special message for his people. The *Jungmädel* leaders had urged all the members to listen to their Führer tonight. Korinna always looked forward to hearing his radio broadcasts. She only wished she could see him speak in person.

For the rest of the half hour, Korinna sat in front of the radio listening to the Führer's voice. At first the speech was quiet yet forceful, but soon the voice took on a moving ring. By the end of the speech, Adolf Hitler spoke at the top of his voice, over the cheers of his followers. What he said was always the same: Destroy the enemy, the Jews and the radical intellectuals, and out of the misery they were now in, a stronger more unified Germany would ascend. A Germany without poverty, without unemployment. The Third Reich that would last for one thousand years!

At the end of the speech, Korinna dropped her kitten on the sofa and stood up as it scurried out of the room. She lifted her right arm in a smart salute. *"Heil Hitler!"* She looked expectantly at her mother.

Frau Rehme, sitting on the sofa and darning one of her husband's socks, looked up at her daughter. *"Heil Hitler,"* she murmured, then she went back to her sewing.

Korinna smiled and sat down next to her mother. "Isn't the Führer wonderful?"

"Mmmmm," Frau Rehme agreed.

"Mother! Weren't you paying attention to him? His speech was wonderful!"

Frau Rehme shrugged slightly, but Korinna caught the subtle movement and she frowned.

Frau Rehme said, "His speeches are all beginning to sound the same."

"He repeats himself only because he wants us to remember the important things."

"What important things?"

"Who our enemies are, of course, and what we can look forward to when Germany wins the war and becomes the power it once was," Korinna said, repeating the very words her *Jungmädel* leader had said the day before.

"And our Führer is going to do all this?"

"Of course."

Frau Rehme put down her sewing. "At whose expense? At what cost?"

Korinna stood up. "Mother, I can't believe you're talking like this!"

Frau Rehme gently reached up and took her daughter's hand. "Sit down, Korinna. I love the Fatherland as much as you, if not more because I've been alive longer. But you mustn't follow blindly behind great promises."

Korinna allowed her mother to pull her down beside her. "Mother, how can you question the Führer? Someone might report you."

"Is that the only reason it's wrong to question what one man is saying? Fear?"

"It's not fear, Mother," Korinna said impatiently. "It's love and respect. I have nothing to fear from anyone, because I'm a loyal German, just like you, Mother. And you should never question the Führer, because he's only doing what's best for us."

Korinna's mother didn't say anything. She picked up her darning and once again began to sew.

Korinna sat silently, watching her mother for a few moments. Finally she said, "Rita is going to tell our leaders about her cousin, Elsa Demmer."

"Her own cousin," Frau Rehme said with a sigh, shaking her head.

"Elsa said she felt sorry for our enemies."

"Who? The English? The French?"

Korinna picked impatiently at a loose thread on the couch. "No, the Jews."

Suddenly, they heard a muffled crash upstairs. "What was that?" Korinna whispered, afraid to move. She noticed her mother's face looked pale, as though she had put on too much powder.

"Stay here," her mother whispered firmly. She stood up and walked out of the room.

Korinna heard her mother make her way stealthily up the stairs. Then only silence. Korinna didn't move. She strained her ears to hear anything at all. Had someone managed to break in upstairs? Had someone crept in the front door while they had been listening to the radio?

"Korinna!"

Korinna jumped up when her mother called. She raced upstairs. Her mother stood in the larger bedroom, looking at a fallen brass figurine, which normally sat on her father's desk. She cuddled Korinna's kitten.

Frau Rehme smiled. "This little rascal is into mischief already. I don't think she'll be playing with this statue any more."

Korinna bent down and picked up the heavy brass figure and placed it back on the desk. Taking the kitten from her mother, she said, "She must be pretty strong to have knocked that thing onto the floor."

Frau Rehme nodded in agreement.

Just then they heard the back door open.

"Hello," Herr Rehme called, stomping the snow off his boots. "I'm home!"

Korinna and her mother hurried downstairs to the kitchen.

Frau Rehme reached up to give her tall husband a kiss on his smooth cheek. "Couldn't you have come in the front door where we have a mat for all this snow?"

"The back door was more convenient," he said shortly. He glanced down at his wife, and she said nothing more about it.

"Hi, Papa," Korinna said, thinking the back door was rather *inconvenient*. It led out to a narrow back alley, which ran between the tightly packed houses at the edge of the city until it finally emptied out onto a seldomly used road. This road was bordered by occasional houses on one side and a thick forest on the other, and it led immediately out of the city. "Why did the school have such a late meeting?" she asked.

"How about a kiss first?" her father teased, bending over. "The meeting was nothing, just some things we had to go over," he said casually.

Korinna took her father's coat. "Was it about Fräulein Meiser?"

"No." He snapped his scarf over the high back of a kitchen chair and strode into the front room.

Korinna glanced at her mother, who avoided her eyes but took the coat from her arms. She left to hang it up. Korinna followed her father into the front room. He sat in his chair with his feet up on a stool, his head back, eyes closed, and a smoking pipe clamped between his teeth. He should have looked restful, but he didn't. He opened his eyes slightly to look at his daughter as Korinna sat down on the opposite couch.

He removed the pipe from his mouth. "Sometimes it's not good to ask too many questions. You could ask the wrong thing to the wrong person."

"But I just want to know what happened to Fräulein Meiser. She was my favorite teacher."

"And she was a good friend," her father replied. "I'll tell you what little I know, Korinna. But you mustn't talk about her to anyone else. Promise?"

Korinna nodded.

"Last night the Gestapo went to her house to arrest her father. She refused to let him go without her. She went with him."

Korinna gasped. "You mean she didn't even *have* to go? She *wanted* to?"

"Her father is old. He may be dying. I expect she wants to be with him in case he needs her. Except, I'm afraid she'll find that she'll be separated from her father after all."

"Why?"

"I doubt they keep the men and women together in those work camps," Herr Rehme said.

Korinna shook her head sadly. "Then she went for nothing."

"It wasn't exactly for nothing, Korinna."

"Then for what?"

Herr Rehme shrugged. "For love? I don't know, Korinna, maybe there's something even more important than that."

Korinna silently agreed that love was important. It was love for the Fatherland that had made her turn in her notes on Fräulein Meiser last week. And she loved her parents, and she knew her parents loved her. What could be more important than love?

She couldn't imagine.

"Why was Fräulein Meiser's father arrested?" she finally asked.

"I don't know, and I think it's best not to find out," her father said somberly. Then his face brightened slightly as he smiled at his daughter. "Don't you have any schoolwork to do?"

Korinna stood up. "Yes." She walked over and gave her father a hug. "I'm glad your home, Papa."

"I am too, Korinna." He gave her a fierce hug. "Now, go do your homework."

Korinna kissed her mother in the kitchen, then went upstairs. Her kitten was sleeping in the middle of her bed. She stroked the silky head once, then picked up her book bag which sat neatly by the side of her bed. For a moment she just stood there. Hadn't she left her bag next to the *Schrank*? She always left her bag in the same place, next to the wardrobe, not next to the bed. She shrugged. Her mother must have moved it for some reason. If she thought of it, she'd ask her about it later.

She took out her books and sat down quietly at her desk, deciding which subject to tackle first. Then she heard it—a soft rhythmic noise that sounded like something trapped behind her wall. Her heart started to race.

It was the mice in her walls. They weren't gone after all! She turned to her bed and saw her kitten stretching and washing its paws.

Korinna's heart pounded so hard it felt like it was more in the middle of her throat than in her chest somewhere. If only she could find the mouse hole. Her kitten would surely scare the mice away for good!

She decided the noise seemed to be coming from the middle of her wall. Holding her breath, she pushed away from her desk and tiptoed to her wardrobe. She crouched down. The back panel of the *Schrank* almost came down to the floor against the wall. Maybe she'd find a concealed mouse hole back there, she thought. Carefully, she pressed her shoulder against the heavy wooden piece of furniture. It wouldn't budge. She pushed again. Nothing. It couldn't be that heavy, she thought with despair. She knew if she could just move her wardrobe, she would find the source of her mouse noises.

Korinna straightened up and faced the front of the *Schrank*. She placed one trembling hand on either side of it and pulled. Finally it seemed to be moving! She tugged a little harder, and the wardrobe moved silently away from the wall a bit more, but only on the right side.

The mouse noises stopped. She grabbed her kitten and clutched the squirming animal in her arms. With a thudding heart, she peered around the right back-side of the piece of furniture. But there wasn't a little mouse hole leading into the wall—practically the entire wall behind her wardrobe was missing!

Korinna thought her heart would explode in her throat. She dropped her kitten. Frantically she slammed her shoulder against her wardrobe to close up the gaping, black void.

That was no mouse hole—there was something much bigger hiding back there! She had smelled the rank smell of unwashed bodies, and she had seen the pale glow of skin, and the gleam of eyes.

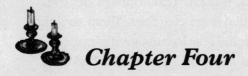

Chapter Four

Feet pounded up the narrow stairs, and her parents burst into the room. *"Liebling,* what is it? Stop screaming!" Her mother wrapped her up in her arms.

Korinna took a sobbing breath. She hadn't even realized she was screaming. She pointed a shaky finger. "Back there! Something's back there!"

"Hush, hush," her mother crooned.

Korinna tried to pull out of her mother's arms. Her father pulled the thick curtain over the window. The room was dark until he lit a couple candles.

Korinna scrubbed away the tears on her cheeks, wondering why her father didn't just turn on the overhead light. "Monsters, Papa! I have monsters behind my wall!" Her stomach churned with fear.

"It's not monsters, *Liebling,"* Herr Rehme said softly. He looked at his wife and his shoulders sagged as though he carried some great weight. "Those are people back there."

A fierce dread washed over her, strangling her. Korinna gasped for air.

"Jews," her mother said, still holding her daughter's shoulders. She gave them a little shake. "Did you hear me, Korinna?"

Korinna nodded mutely. Tears burned her eyes, and her fingers ached from clenching them so tightly.

With a heavy sigh, Herr Rehme gently pulled the *Schrank* away from the wall. The candles flickered with the movement. The wardrobe moved silently. Now Korinna could see someone had carefully hinged it to the wall on the left side in such a way that the hinges were invisible from anywhere in her room. Only when someone pulled the wardrobe away from the wall were the hinges visible. Also, the hinges held the wardrobe a millimeter off the floor so its legs wouldn't rub noisily on the wooden boards.

When her father completely "opened" up the wardrobe, Korinna once again stared at the gaping hole in her bedroom wall. Even knowing it was not monsters hiding in the blackness did nothing to calm her heartbeat.

Jews were worse.

Korinna's mother crouched down next to the opening, which was half as tall as the shoulder high wardrobe. Korinna and her father stood behind her.

"Sophie, it's okay. This is Korinna, my daughter," Frau Rehme said gently.

A pale face, creased with lines of worry and fatigue, inched into the candlelight. Sophie's thin neck ended in a drab green coat collar, which added a green pallor to her skin. Her dark and suspicious eyes stared up at them. "She's the Nazi?" Her voice came out rough and crumbly, as if she didn't use it much.

Ignoring the question, Frau Rehme said to Korinna, "This is Sophie Krugmann, and this is her daughter Rachel, who's five."

Rachel had a mass of curly hair that tumbled to her shoulders. Her wide eyes roamed the room and finally fell on Korinna. She smiled. Korinna glared at her until the little girl pulled back into the shadows, her smile gone, lips trembling.

Sophie hugged her daughter close and kissed the top of her head. When she looked up again, her eyes shone with unshed tears. "Are we safe with her knowing we're here?"

Herr Rehme said, "It's too dangerous to move you right now. Maybe in a week or two, but right now . . ." His voice trailed off as he placed a hand on his daughter's shoulder. "Right now we have no choice."

Sophie turned to her young daughter and said, "I told you to wait until later." Then she looked at Korinna's mother. "I told Rachel to wait, but she gets so restless with nothing to do and no one to play with. She likes to walk back and forth, back and forth."

So that's what she had heard, Korinna thought, staring into the shadows. It had sounded like a trapped animal.

Frau Rehme smiled with understanding. "It's all right, Sophie."

"But now she knows," Sophie said, nodding
toward Korinna, her voice weary and tinged with fear.

"She was bound to find out sooner or later," Herr
Rehme said.

Sophie took a deep breath and looked up at
Korinna. "Do you love your parents?" she demanded.

Startled by the direct question, Korinna could only
nod her head.

"Then don't report them. I know you hate us—you've learned to hate Jews in school and at your meetings. But don't take it out on your parents. They'll be shot as traitors," Sophie said bluntly, her dark eyes drilling into Korinna's light blue ones.

"That's enough, Sophie," Korinna's mother said firmly. "Do you need more blankets?"

Sophie shook her head and moved back into the darkness, to join her daughter.

"*Gute Nacht,*" Korinna's father said as he pushed the wardrobe back into place.

"Good night," Sophie replied softly before the hole was completely covered up.

Korinna sat stiffly on the side of her bed. Her mother sat next to her, and her father leaned back against the *Schrank*. The candles burned behind him, leaving his face in shadow.

"Make them leave!" Korinna cried, a tight ball of anger and fear constricting her throat. "Get rid of them!"

Herr Rehme shook his head. "You heard what I said, Korinna. It's too dangerous right now. The Gestapo has been searching houses and making many arrests lately. The man who owns the next hiding place the Krugmanns are going to thinks it's too risky right now to move them. The Krugmanns have to stay."

Korinna crossed her arms to ward off a chill that left her trembling. "How long have they been here?"

"Only a few days."

"So they were the mouse noises I heard," Korinna said through tight lips.

Korinna stiffened as her mother reached out and patted her back. "We felt it was best not to say anything to you. We know how involved you are in your *Jungmädel*. We thought you might . . . ," her mother paused and looked at her husband. "We thought you might not like the idea."

But Korinna knew what her mother had been about to say. They had thought she might report them for the good of the Fatherland. And she should. She had to. For the Fatherland. For the Führer!

"Sophie's husband and another daughter, Ruth— she's fourteen—are staying somewhere else," her father said, leaning forward to brush his fingers across her cheek.

Korinna ducked her father's hand and moved stiffly to sit closer to the head of her bed. "Why couldn't they all stay in the same place? Someplace else," she added vehemently.

Her mother sighed. "There's barely enough room back there for the two of them. Luckily Rachel is small. Like our place, most hiding places aren't big enough."

"And are too dangerous," her father added.

Her parents moved toward the door. Her father turned around and said, "Korinna, you mustn't say anything about this to anyone. Many lives are at stake. Do you understand?"

Korinna looked at her hands tightly clasped in her lap. It was her duty as a loyal German to say something—didn't her parents realize that? Her parents were traitors! Why couldn't it have been Rita's parents, or Eva's parents?

"Korinna?" her mother prodded.

Korinna closed her eyes, trying to ignore them. How could she promise anything? She was so confused. Her parents were harboring Jews right here, *right behind her own bedroom wall!* If she didn't report them she'd be a traitor, too!

Korinna heard her door close with a quiet click as her parents left her room. Lying down on her stomach, she nestled her head in her arms.

Her parents were traitors.

Traitors were shot.

 *Chapter Five*

For a long time, Korinna tossed and turned as the candles burned lower and lower. She was afraid to be without the light, knowing the enemy was so close. She could hardly believe she had been sleeping peacefully these last few nights with hated Jews so near. Now that she knew what was on the other side of her wall, she'd never be able to sleep easily again.

When the candles finally burned out, Korinna's eyes were still open. She slipped out from under her warm blankets and tiptoed over to the window. Pushing open the curtain, she hoped there would be some moonlight to light up her room, but the sky was black. Even the snow on the ground looked black. Korinna shivered in the cold air and got back into bed, leaving the curtain open.

When a pale glow filled the room as the morning sun inched over the eastern edge of the city, Korinna finally fell asleep.

When she awoke, the curtain once again covered the window, blocking out most of the sunlight. She heard footsteps come up the stairs and someone knock on her door.

Her mother quietly pushed the door open and peeked in. "Korinna? Are you awake?"

Korinna closed her eyes and lay still. She heard her mother come in the room and place something on the foot of her bed. She smelled warm rye bread and potato and carrot soup. They had gathered plenty of vegetables from their garden during the summer. Korinna's stomach growled. She was just about to "wake up" and thank her mother for bringing up some food for her, when she heard the soft swish of her wardrobe being pulled away from the wall. Korinna grimly realized the food was not for her.

"*Guten Morgen*," Frau Rehme said in a loud whisper, lifting the tray off her daughter's bed.

Korinna heard Sophie grunt an indistinguishable greeting. At least she could be civil, thought Korinna angrily. She didn't like to think of her mother waiting on this rude woman. It was humiliating having her mother serve a hated, thankless Jew.

"Did you sleep well?"

"It was cold," Sophie said with a mouthful of food.

Frau Rehme sighed. "I know. It was colder last

night than it has been in a while. Tonight I'll give you my extra blanket. That should help."

Korinna could barely contain herself. Let the Jews freeze! Her mother shouldn't be giving up her warmth to help the enemy. What was she thinking?

"This soup is very good," Rachel said softly.

"Thank you. It's Korinna's favorite, too."

"Is that the girl I met last night?" Rachel asked.

Korinna guessed her mother nodded, because then Rachel loudly said, "She's pretty!" forgetting to keep her voice down.

"Shhhhh," Sophie hissed.

"Korinna's still sleeping," Frau Rehme whispered. "I don't think she slept very well last night."

"Doesn't she have to go to school?" Rachel asked, her mouth obviously stuffed with something.

"Shhhhh," repeated the little girl's mother.

"Not today," Korinna's mother said. "Today she'll miss school just this once."

"I miss school everyday," Rachel said sadly. "I miss my friends."

"I'm sure you do," Frau Rehme said softly. "But someday soon you'll have many new friends to play with."

Korinna couldn't catch the little girl's reply. But whatever she said had made her mother laugh softly. Korinna realized she hadn't heard her mother laugh very much lately. Jealousy burned in her empty stomach.

". . . what will she do?" It was Sophie speaking. Korinna had missed some of the question, but she knew immediately the Jew referred to her.

"I hope she'll do the right thing," said Korinna's mother, pausing. "But she's very involved in her *Jungmädel* and she honestly believes . . . well, they teach her many things at those meetings," Frau Rehme said, sounding apologetic.

"Why do you let her go?" Sophie asked.

"We have no choice. If she didn't join the group, she would be made to join anyway, and she'd be watched with suspicion. And Bernd and I, too, would be watched more closely. It's best that everyone thinks we're loyal to the Führer, then they don't suspect us of helping Jews."

"They've lied to her," Sophie stated flatly.

Her mother sighed and started to reply.

Korinna fumed. How dare her mother speak about her to this horrible Jew! And what did Sophie know about the wonderful things they did at *Jungmädel* meetings? Her *Jungmädel* leaders didn't lie to her. At the meetings she learned patriotic songs, she baked, she hiked outside, she made friends, and she even got to march in parades. They listened to the Führer's speeches, which filled them with pride for their Fatherland. If anyone had lied to her, it was her very own parents!

She was so angry she missed the rest of the conversation. All she heard was her mother reminding the

Krugmanns to be quiet. Then the wardrobe tapped lightly into place.

She lay very still, too upset to talk to her mother. She wanted to talk to someone about all the awful things that were going on in her house, namely the Krugmanns, but that person couldn't be her mother. Obviously, her mother wouldn't understand. Maybe she could talk to Rita.

Korinna heard her mother step softly to her side. A cool hand brushed the hair off her forehead, and a kiss as light as a sigh was left on her cheek. Then her mother left.

Korinna wiped the kiss away. Her mother was a traitor. How could she ever love her mother or father again the way she used to, knowing they weren't loyal Germans? Tears slipped through her tightly shut eyelids and slid across her nose and down onto the pillow. Why did things have to get so terrible? Why did her parents have to change?

Actually, they hadn't changed, she realized miserably. They had always been traitors. She'd just never known it.

When Korinna opened her eyes again, the curtain was open wide and the brilliant, snowy sunlight from outside burst into her room. She stretched. Her stomach growled. Throwing back her blankets, she sat up and swung her legs out of bed. Her clothes hung wrinkled and twisted on her body like the trunk of a gnarled tree. Glancing nervously at her wardrobe, she quickly changed into a wool skirt and an old blue sweater. Anger filled her. It wasn't right to feel so uncomfortable in her own room.

Downstairs, Korinna found her mother sitting at the kitchen table peeling potatoes. She smiled brightly when Korinna walked into the room.

"So you've finally decided to get up!" she teased.

Korinna shrugged. She longed to go to her mother and hug her and beg her to get rid of the Jews and become a loyal German, but she knew it would do no good. "I guess I was very tired. You should have gotten me up for school, though."

"It won't hurt to miss one day, Korinna. You work hard and do well in school. Rita stopped by to see you after school. I told her you were sick."

Knowing her best friend had stopped by to see her made her feel a little better. At least she could count on Rita.

Korinna peered into a pot that sat on the small stove.

"I saved some soup for you," her mother said, nodding toward the pot Korinna inspected. "Fresh bread, too."

Normally, Korinna would have asked where the rest of the loaf had gone, but this time she knew. It had gone to feed the enemy.

She served herself some soup and bread and sat down at the table across from her mother.

"Did you sleep well?" her mother asked.

"Fine," Korinna said. The soup, her favorite kind, tasted bland today. Jews had enjoyed it before her and had taken all the flavor and enjoyment out of it. She pushed the bowl away.

"Do you want more? You must be hungry having missed breakfast this morning."

Korinna shook her head and stood up. "I have schoolwork to do," she replied, leaving the kitchen. On her way up the stairs her stomach rumbled fiercely. She tried to ignore the empty feeling in her stomach and in her heart. The Jews had tried to take the Fatherland away from loyal Germans, and now they were trying to take her parents away from her.

In her room, Korinna sat at her desk and stared at her open history book. Even her favorite subject didn't interest her today. She kept glancing at her wardrobe, wondering what those awful Jews were doing back there. She knew there couldn't be a window, or even very much space. What did they do all day? she wondered.

She turned back to her history book. Someday this book would be entirely rewritten, thanks to Adolf Hitler. Hopefully they would take out mention of the Treaty of Versailles as if it had never happened, which, in fact, it never should have. The Treaty of Versailles

was a disgrace to Germany. Imagine Germany
without an army or a navy or an air force! And
Jews, she knew, had played a big part in this humiliation, though she wasn't quite sure exactly which part.
But thanks to the Führer, Germany would be the
power it had been before the last war, which they
had somehow lost. She knew Germany would now
win back its pride and power as long as the enemy,
the Jews, were kept out of the way. Traitors, like her
parents, too.

———————

Korinna finished her schoolwork as the last feeble rays
of the late winter sun filtered into her room, leaving it
a muddy shade of rose. She shivered in the cool air.
She stood up and stretched. It was hard to sit in one
position for so long.

As she shrugged her shoulders to relieve the tension, she heard the sound she had once believed to be
mice trapped in her walls. Now that she knew what
the sound really was, though, she didn't know how
she ever could have thought it was mice. The sound
was obviously rhythmic. Not the erratic scrambling of
mice, but the even pace of someone walking back and
forth. Step, step, step, turn. Step, step, step, turn. It
must be a very small room, she thought. She started
to walk in time to the sound of the steps. Step, step,
step, turn. A *very* small room.

"Korinna," Frau Rehme called from downstairs.

Korinna opened her door and looked down to her mother standing at the foot of the stairs. "Yes?"

"Will you come down and help me?"

Korinna walked downstairs, following her mother into the kitchen. "What are you cooking?" she asked, spying her kitten curled up next to her milk bowl.

Her mother pointed to the two pots on the stove. "Potatoes here for the Krugmanns, and potatoes with cheese sauce in this pot for our supper."

"Why do you have to cook separately for them?" Korinna asked, not able to bring herself to say their name.

"The Krugmanns keep kosher."

Korinna knew that the word *kosher* had something to do with the Krugmann's religion, but she didn't know what, and she didn't care.

"Kosher means they have to keep dairy products and meat separate. There's milk and cheese with our potatoes so I have to cook them in a different pot. The Krugmanns will have plain potatoes and a little bit of beef."

Korinna stared at her mother. "That's stupid!" she exclaimed.

Frau Rehme set down her wooden spoon with an abrupt snap. "People have a right to their beliefs, Korinna," she said sharply.

"But you shouldn't be working so hard for them, Mother. Why are you cooking them such a big, hot supper anyway? What's wrong with the bread and cheese or plain leftovers we usually have?"

"It's so chilly outside, I thought some hot food would help warm them up before the long cold night."

"But they're only Jews!" Korinna protested.

"They're people," her mother said, suddenly sounding weary.

"They're the enemy," Korinna countered stubbornly, "and they shouldn't be here. You shouldn't be waiting on them the way you are."

Frau Rehme waved the wooden spoon. "Korinna, they have nothing. Should I take away their religion, too? It's no hardship for me to try to cook for them in a kosher manner, so why shouldn't I? And why shouldn't I make them a hot meal?"

Korinna sat on a chair and pinched her lips together. It was no use talking to her mother.

Frau Rehme sighed. "Take this tray." She handed her daughter a tray with two bowls full of potatoes. She carried a tray with beef and carrots and glasses for water or milk. She walked to the kitchen door and looked back. "Are you coming?" her mother asked.

Korinna calmly stood and carried the tray, following her mother up the stairs. On the outside, she knew she appeared obedient and reserved. But inside, anger roiled in her stomach like a pot of boiling soup. What was she doing? Now *she* was serving the enemy, waiting on them as if she were a servant or a slave!

Staring at her mother's back, she had a strong urge to drop the tray she carried. It would make a mess—a mess she would gladly clean up. Anything was better than catering to these Jews, the hated enemy of the Fatherland.

But, instead, she quietly followed her mother into her bedroom, the tray still balanced carefully in her hands. Her mother pulled the wardrobe away from the wall, and Korinna smelled the cloud of confined air rush out at her—the musty smell of burning wax, stale breath, a full chamber pot, and unwashed bodies. It was the despicable stink of Jews, Korinna thought, trying to hold her breath.

Frau Rehme took the tray from Korinna and passed it in to the Krugmanns.

"Thank you," Sophie said, sniffing the food appreciatively. "It looks and smells wonderful. You're getting better at keeping things kosher," she added.

Korinna's mother smiled. "I'm learning."

Sophie returned the smile. *"Danke."* It was the first smile Korinna had seen from this woman, but it quickly disappeared as she glanced up from the opening to Korinna, standing behind her mother. She wished she had on her *Jungmädel* uniform.

In the failing light, Korinna noticed the heavy circles under Frau Krugmann's dark eyes. And her thin face looked wan, almost the color of her faded yellow bedroom walls.

"Later I'll bring up some hot water for you to bathe with," Frau Rehme offered. "Give me your chamber pot and I'll empty it now."

Korinna nearly gagged as Frau Krugmann passed the lidded pot out to her mother. She couldn't bear the thought of her mother cleaning it for these abhorrent Jews. It was more than humiliating, it was hateful. But all she could do was watch as her mother lifted the heavy pot and went into the bathroom with it.

Korinna watched Frau Krugmann eat. Should she push the wardrobe back in place, or was her mother coming right back? What if someone unexpectedly stopped by the house—would he hear the *Schrank* being pushed back into place and wonder about it? She looked toward the window. Shouldn't the curtain be closed in case the Schlossers happened to look out their back window and into hers? Quickly she moved to the window and pulled the heavy curtain closed so her neighbors wouldn't find out they lived near traitors. She clenched her teeth.

"Hello."

Korinna looked back at the opening in the wall. The little girl with the curly hair poked her head out. Now Korinna could see that the hidden room glowed with candlelight.

"Hello," Korinna said gruffly.

"Do you remember me?" the little girl asked shyly.

Korinna nodded briefly.

"My name's Rachel. I think your hair is very pretty."

Korinna didn't say anything. She didn't want this little Jewess saying nice things to her. She turned away from the wardrobe and faced her desk.

"Are you doing homework?" the little girl asked.

Korinna shook her head without turning around. She lit the candle her father had left on her desk.

"Mama, look," Rachel said. "Her hair shines like that statue we used to have in our front hall."

"Yes, darling, just like bronze," Frau Krugmann agreed softly. "Now scoot back and leave her alone."

Korinna heard her mother walk in with the washed out chamber pot. "Here you go, Sophie," she said. "I'll leave the wardrobe open to give you some fresh air, and in a little while I'll bring up that hot water."

"Do you have any more paper, Frau Rehme?" Rachel asked quickly.

Korinna's mother paused slightly. "Perhaps my daughter has some she could give you, Rachel."

Korinna frowned. She didn't want to give anything away to a Jew, not even paper.

"Fräulein?" Rachel asked. "Do you have a little paper for me?"

Korinna hastily pinched a few sheets from her supply and, turning around, thrust them at the girl. "Here."

"Oh, thank you," Rachel gushed, her pale face lighting up with her smile. "Thank you, thank you, thank you!"

"What do you want them for?" Korinna asked before she could stop herself.

"I like to draw," Rachel said. "Like this." She disappeared for a second, then reappeared with a sheaf of paper clutched in her hand. "See?" She held the small bundle of paper toward Korinna. The drawings were all done with a gray pencil, so they looked rather dull and lifeless.

Korinna knew she could simply turn her back and walk away. She didn't *have* to look at this Jew's drawings, but her hand moved forward anyway. She took the bundle and pulled off the string that held it together.

"The first one is my house," Rachel explained.

The house had flowers in front of it and someone in each window, waving.

"Can I show her?" Rachel asked Korinna's mother.

Frau Rehme glanced at the curtained window. "You may come out," she said, "but Korinna has to crouch down so the people outside don't see a lot of shadows moving about."

Korinna scowled at her mother. She had more important things to do than to look at these ugly drawings. She tried to catch her mother's eyes, but her mother didn't seem to notice.

Rachel crawled on all fours over to Korinna, and squatted there until Korinna lowered herself to the floor. Korinna sat cross-legged and Rachel leaned over one of the older girl's knees, pointing to the people in the windows.

"That's my papa. He's with Ruth staying somewhere else. And that's Ruth, my older sister. There's Mama and that's me," she said, pointing to a face surrounded by curly hair. "My hair is like my papa's."

"This is Ruth playing the piano," Rachel continued, pulling another drawing from the pile. "She is very, very, very good. She wants to play the piano when she grows up and make people pay to come hear her play. But she said I don't have to pay." Rachel extracted another drawing. "And this is the apple tree in our yard. The flowers are pretty, but the apples are sour." She made a sour face.

Korinna bit the inside of her lip, stopping her smile just in time.

Rachel explained every drawing in her pile, and Korinna couldn't help noticing the wistful expression that sometimes overcame the girl's otherwise cheerful exuberance. She had more pictures of her house and family, and of her friends and school and synagogue. Some of which, Korinna realized, the little girl would probably never see again. But that didn't bother Korinna. After all, these were Jews, one of the enemies to the Fatherland, and they deserved to suffer.

"My husband will be home soon," said Korinna's mother. She had been sitting on her daughter's bed, watching. "You'd better get back inside in case he brings someone home with him. Sometimes he's obliged to invite someone over for supper at the last minute," she explained.

Rachel scrambled back into the hideaway with her drawings and her new paper.

"I'll bring your water up now, before we eat," Frau Rehme said.

"Don't rush," Sophie said. "Take care of your family first. We're not going anywhere," she added wryly.

Korinna's mother smiled at the attempted joke and closed the wardrobe against the wall. She shook her head. "It's amazing how that woman still can hold her head up and find humor in her situation after all she's been through." She stacked the two trays of empty dishes.

"Do you need help carrying those downstairs?" Korinna asked, ignoring the comment about the Jewess.

"No, thank you, Korinna, you've helped enough today," Frau Rehme said thoughtfully. "You've helped more than you know."

Korinna scowled. She didn't want any thanks for

being a traitor to her Fatherland. She felt guilty enough as it was, without her mother rubbing it in. She sat down at her desk and pretended to study until she heard her mother leave the room. Then step, step, step, turn. Rachel was walking behind the wall again. Korinna slammed her book shut, creating a loud cracking sound like a gunshot she'd once heard. The walking stopped. Korinna quickly left her room and sat alone in the quiet of the front room until her father came home for supper.

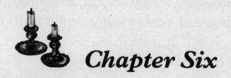

Chapter Six

"Korinna, you've never not wanted to go to school," Frau Rehme said, frowning.

Korinna buried her face in her pillow. "I don't feel well," she mumbled.

"You missed yesterday. You must go today," her mother insisted.

Korinna felt like screaming. Didn't her mother understand that she couldn't just go to school as if everything were normal? Rita would take one look at her and know she was hiding something. "I don't feel well!"

Now Korinna's mother began to sound angry. "It will look suspicious if you suddenly start to miss school. You're not sick, and you know it. Get out of bed now or you'll be late to meet Rita."

Korinna groaned.

"Now." Her mother turned away from the bed and left the room.

Korinna reluctantly flipped back her blankets and shivered in the cold air. She looked toward her wardrobe. Were the Krugmanns up yet? Maybe they slept most of the day since there wasn't much they could possibly do back there.

Quickly she got dressed. Her kitten, still unnamed, darted between her legs and kept swinging at the hem of her skirt.

"Ouch!" Korinna exclaimed as the little rascal missed her skirt and dug a sharp claw into her leg. She bent down and picked up the kitten, hugging her close to her face. "You silly thing," she said softly. The kitten began to purr as she stroked its fuzzy head. "I'll play with you after school," she promised as she deposited her new pet on her bed and gathered her schoolbooks.

Downstairs she finished a hurried breakfast and then went to say good-bye to her mother who stood by the stove, cooking. Korinna didn't look in the pots; she knew the food was for the Jews upstairs. Didn't they do anything but eat? she wondered, annoyed to find her mother working so hard for the enemy. It was a miracle she hadn't noticed all the extra cooking her mother had been doing lately, she thought.

Frau Rehme hugged her daughter. "Have a good day at school, Korinna."

Korinna hugged her mother back. "I love you, Mother." And she thought, but you're a traitor to the Fatherland—I have to turn you in. Abruptly she pulled out of her mother's arms. "I'm late," she said and left the house.

Rita was waiting impatiently at the corner. "Are you feeling better?" she asked.

Korinna nodded. She didn't dare say anything for fear that the whole horrible story would spill out.

"Good," said Rita. "Now we'd better hurry so we won't be late. Eva went on ahead."

The two girls walked quickly down the sidewalk. It hadn't snowed in a couple of days, and the sidewalks were pretty clear of snow and ice.

"Guess what?" Rita asked, excitement charging her voice.

"What?"

Rita stopped walking and turned to her friend. "The Führer is coming! There's going to be a big parade, and our *Jungmädel* gets to march in it!"

Excitement fluttered through Korinna's stomach. "Here?" she exclaimed. "To our city? How wonderful!"

Rita nodded, a big smile spreading across her face. "In three weeks. We're going to make a special banner and Fräulein Schönwald is going to write a new song for the occasion."

Korinna walked along silently.

"What's wrong?" Rita asked, looking at her friend from the corners of her eyes.

"Nothing," Korinna said quickly.

"I thought you'd be more excited about the news."

"I am excited," Korinna said. "It's just that . . . that there's a lot to do by then," she mumbled.

Rita waved her hand. "Oh, don't worry about that.

We're going to meet everyday until then just to get ready."

"Great," Korinna said, relieved that they had reached the school building.

"I'll talk to you at break," Rita said as they entered their classroom.

For a second, Korinna was startled not to see Fräulein Meiser, until she remembered that she had been taken to a work camp with her aging father. Korinna shook her head. She couldn't understand how her teacher could have done something like that. Not that the work camps were supposed to be all that bad, but still, to give up her job and her home. It didn't make sense to her.

"How are you feeling?" Eva whispered as Korinna sat down next to her.

"Better, thanks," she replied.

"Are you sure you're feeling okay?"

Korinna turned to her with a frown. "Yes, why?"

Eva shrugged. "You look pale and tired."

"I haven't been sleeping well lately," Korinna said truthfully.

"Maybe you should have stayed home another day," Eva suggested.

"Maybe, but my mother wouldn't let me." She smiled wanly. "You know mothers."

Eva smiled back. "I know. I have one, too."

Not like mine, thought Korinna. Mine is a traitor. She turned her attention back to the lesson, but she found it hard to concentrate. She couldn't help wondering what the Krugmanns were doing.

Finally school was over. She met Rita and Eva in the usual spot to the right of the large front doors of the school building.

"Okay, let's go," Rita said cheerfully. "You'll eat dinner at my house and then we'll go to the meeting."

"I'm not going," Korinna said.

Both Rita and Eva stared at her with surprise. "What do you mean you're not going?" Rita demanded.

Korinna lifted a hand to her head. "I still don't feel very well. It kind of came back during school."

"What is it?" Rita asked. "A cold? A headache? What?"

"A little of both," Korinna said evasively. "I . . . I haven't been sleeping well lately."

"Is it the mice?" Rita asked.

"No, no!" Korinna said a bit too forcefully. She'd forgotten that she'd told her friends about the noises. But why wouldn't she have? Friends shared everything from gossip about her cute neighbor, Alfred Bissle, to rustling mouse noises in the walls. "My father put out a trap to kill them. I haven't heard anything since."

Eva made a face. "I wouldn't want mice in my walls."

"It was nothing," Korinna said hastily. "They're gone now."

"That's good," Eva said. "I'd hate to have something behind my bedroom wall making scary noises. Especially little mice with their beady pink eyes and those awful rat tails."

Rita nodded in agreement.

Korinna groaned inwardly. If only they knew the truth, she thought. Perhaps they'd think Jews were preferable to mice. After all, Jews didn't have beady pink eyes, they had dark, suspicious eyes.

Rita nudged her. "Korinna! Are you falling asleep on your feet?"

Korinna nodded. "I am really tired. I guess I should go home now." She was eager to get away from her friends' prying eyes and questions. "Tomorrow you can tell me about the plans for the parade." Waving, she turned away and started home alone.

Ten minutes later, she turned up the narrow path to her small red brick house with the green painted door and shutters. It was a pretty house, she decided, with window boxes full of flowers in the summer and icicles hanging from the roof in the winter.

Entering the house, she called to her mother who answered from the front room. Korinna was glad her mother didn't spend all her time with the Jews. It was bad enough she cooked and cared for them.

Korinna's mother looked up. She held a dress in one hand and a needle and thread in the other. "How was school?"

Korinna sat down beside her mother. "Long," she

said with a sigh. She fingered the familiar material her mother was working on. "What are you doing?"

Her mother held up the dress. "Do you recognize it?"

Korinna nodded. It was one of her dresses that she had long since grown out of. "Why did you keep that?"

"I kept most of your dresses to pass on to my grandchildren."

Korinna laughed. "I don't think you have to mend any of my old dresses just yet."

Her mother's face suddenly turned serious. "This one isn't for my future granddaughter. This one is for Rachel."

"Rachel?" Korinna repeated, stunned. "The Jew?"

"Rachel, the little girl upstairs who only has one dress to her name," her mother corrected.

"But that's my dress," Korinna protested.

"It doesn't fit you anymore."

"But it's mine," she insisted.

"Then take it!" Frau Rehme threw down the dress and stalked out of the room.

Korinna picked up the dress and held it against herself. Looking down, she had trouble remembering where she had gotten it. Then she remembered. Frau Rosen had made it for her for her fifth birthday. Frau Rosen, whom she had called Auntie long ago, had disappeared. She remembered the day not too long ago that she had walked past the Rosen home and seen the front door wide open. That's when she had known they were gone. But where, she didn't know. Of course that was long after she had stopped talking to Frau Rosen anyway.

She put down the dress and went upstairs. She could hear her mother banging pots and dishes in the kitchen.

In her room, Korinna put her book bag on the floor and called, "Here kitty, kitty." There was no answering meow. "Here kitty, kitty," she called again. Again there was no reply. Or was there? Standing perfectly still, she thought she could hear a faint answering meow. It came from behind her *Schrank*!

Instantly, blind fury flooded her body. The Jews had her kitten! She yanked the wardrobe away from the wall, surprised at how easily and quietly it moved now that she knew what she was doing. Rachel stared up at her from the hole in the wall, cuddling a little bundle of black and white fur.

Korinna reached down and snatched her kitten from the little girl's thin arms. Rachel cried out. Two red scratches welled with blood where the kitten's claws had scraped on the child's forearms.

"She's mine," Korinna said coldly.

Rachel looked up at her with wide eyes, tears streaming down her pale cheeks.

"Come," Sophie said, pulling her daughter into her arms. The woman glared furiously up at Korinna. "You have what's yours, now leave us alone," she commanded.

Korinna scowled at her. What right did this Jewess have, bossing her around? It was her room and her wall and her kitten! These Jews had no rights, didn't they know that? She furiously shoved the wardrobe closed with a loud bang. The kitten, startled by the sudden noise, scrambled out of her hands and darted out of the room.

"Korinna, what's going on?" her mother demanded, practically tripping over the kitten on her way into the bedroom.

"That little Jewess had my kitten."

"Her name is Rachel," her mother said angrily. "I heard her crying. Why is she crying?"

"The kitten scratched her."

"Why?"

Korinna threw up her hands. "Why are you questioning me like this? She had my kitten and I took her back. Papa gave her to me. The kitten is mine!"

"Yes, I know," her mother replied, her voice terse with anger. "Just like the dress is yours, and this room is yours, and this country is yours. You have everything, Korinna. Rachel has nothing! Is it so terrible that she wants to play with *your* kitten? Well, is it?" she demanded when her daughter didn't respond.

Korinna stared at her mother. Salty tears stung her nose and made her eyes water. Her mother had never yelled at her like this before. And now, all because of a Jew, she had suddenly turned against her.

After a tense moment of silence, the anger seemed to flow out of Korinna's mother, and slowly she deflated. Her shoulders sagged as if her spine had lost its strength, and even her face seemed to droop. Finally she just shook her head and left the room.

Korinna flung herself onto her bed. She would have been better off going to her meeting than coming home to this, she thought angrily. Something tickled her hand. Looking, she saw that her kitten had come back and was rubbing against her hand for attention. She sat up and hugged the kitten close.

"So what do you do all day?" she asked her kitten softly. "Do you get lonely with no friends to play with?" She remembered as a child talking to her dolls in much the same way. She had always longed for a little sister, or even a brother, but instead she had grown up with only her dolls to keep her company. Now she had a kitten, but she also had friends and school and *Jungmädel* meetings to fill her time. Her mother's words echoed in her mind, *Rachel has nothing!*

She stroked the kitten's head. "Is the little Jewess fun to play with? Does she keep you company?" she said aloud. It occurred to her that she hadn't been able to find her kitten the other day because Rachel probably had been playing with it.

She tried to imagine what it must be like for the little girl living in a small room, never seeing the sunlight. There would be no toys or games for her to play with, and no friends or outings. She didn't even have any dresses to choose from. Nothing.

The kitten started to wiggle, so Korinna let go of it. It jumped off the bed and walked back and forth in front of the right side of the wardrobe, purring.

Not giving herself a chance to think, Korinna got off the bed. She pulled open the right side of the

Schrank, just a few centimeters. With her foot, she tapped the kitten in the right direction. The kitten pounced through the gaping hole and was swallowed up in the dim glow of candlelight. Korinna slowly pushed the wardrobe back into place.

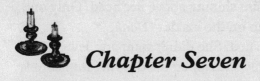

Chapter Seven

Early the next morning, Korinna sat at her desk, her small black book open in front of her.

Biting the end of her pencil, Korinna tried to decide what to write. The last entry she'd made had been about Fräulein Meiser. Now her teacher was gone. How could she turn in her parents? Yet, she knew she must. For the Fatherland. For the Third Reich.

She wrote: "My parents are the enemy."

It was only five words, but she knew it would be enough to interest her *Jungmädel* leaders. Perhaps she would tell them tomorrow, or at least by the next day. The longer she waited, the more she felt like a traitor herself.

Slowly she closed the black notebook and tucked it under her pillow. As she picked up her book bag next to the wardrobe, she noticed a folded piece of paper. Picking it up, she immediately realized it was one of

Rachel's drawings. Thinking it had somehow dropped outside the wardrobe when it had been open, Korinna was about to throw the paper away when she noticed her own name, misspelled, written on the front. She unfolded the paper. Rachel had drawn a picture of the kitten with the sun shining above her head. Only one word was written on the inside—*Danke*.

Korinna frowned. She didn't want any Jews to thank her. Angrily she ripped the drawing into shreds and threw them at her garbage pail next to her desk. Then she raced downstairs.

Thinking about her black book, Korinna had a hard time looking her mother in the eyes as Frau Rehme insisted that Korinna attend the meeting that afternoon. "You haven't gone since you learned of the Krugmanns," her mother argued. "The officers will get suspicious, especially since they're meeting every day now because of the Führer's visit."

"No they won't. Rita's explained to them that I'm still sick."

"Then why are you going to school each day?" her mother asked.

Korinna shifted her heavy book bag on her shoulder. "I get sicker in the afternoon."

Frau Rehme shook her head. "I think you should go," she said sternly, kissing her daughter good-bye.

"Maybe," Korinna said, closing the front door behind her.

Rita met her and they walked to school together as usual.

"Are you coming to the meeting today?" Rita asked.

"It depends on how I feel," Korinna said.

Rita tugged on the strap of her book bag. "You can't be that sick. You sound fine."

Korinna glanced nervously at her best friend. "Don't worry, I'll probably go to the meeting."

"Good, because today we're going to practice the new song for the Führer's visit."

"That sounds like fun," Korinna said. "Rita," she began. "I—I have to tell you something, but you have to promise not to tell anyone."

Rita looked at Korinna obliquely and nodded.

Korinna hesitated. All night she had been debating this question. Should she say something about the Krugmanns to her very best friend? They were supposed to share everything, she had argued with herself.

"Do you promise not to say anything? Not even to Eva?"

"I said I promised," Rita said irritably. "Now tell me!"

Korinna hesitated for a moment. "I—I think I have a crush on Alfred," she blurted out.

Rita stopped walking and confronted her friend. "Are you kidding? That's your big secret? You've had a crush on Alfred for years. What were you really going to tell me?" she asked, her eyes narrowing slightly.

"That's it," Korinna said cheerfully, continuing to

walk toward the school. "I mean I really, really like him. Not just a baby crush, I mean *really*."

Rita skipped to catch up to her friend. "You are lying to me, Korinna. You can't fool me. I've known you too long for that."

They entered the school. "There's Eva, I have to ask her something," Korinna called as she hurried down the hall, leaving Rita staring after her.

———

After school, before Rita had a chance to ask Korinna about that morning, a group of young children raced toward them.

"Jew, Jew, I spit on you!" taunted a group of older boys who chased the young children down the sidewalk. The throng scrambled around and through Korinna and Rita, who were on their way to eat dinner at Rita's house before going to their *Jungmädel* meeting.

Korinna didn't think the seven- and eight-year-olds who raced frantically past her looked all that Jewish. In fact, one of them had pale golden hair, not the thick black hair that she usually associated with Jews. But the yellow stars they were forced to wear gave them away.

Rita grinned. "Come on, Korinna."

"You want to chase those little kids?"

"Sure, why not? They should all be sent away

where they won't disturb anyone. They shouldn't be wandering around these streets, bothering us good, loyal Germans."

"I feel stupid running after a bunch of children," Korinna said, hoping Rita would change her mind.

"Do you feel stupid fighting for Germany?" Rita demanded.

"I would do anything for our Fatherland," Korinna said indignantly. "You know that, Rita."

"Then come on. We have to let those dirty, little Jews know they're not wanted here. Remember, they're the enemy!"

"But they're practically babies!"

Rita's eyes narrowed. "Now you're beginning to sound like Eva."

Korinna looked hard at her best friend. "Okay, let's go," she said. "But we'll have to hurry to catch up." She started to run after the now distant group of children, and she could hear Rita panting behind her.

They finally caught up, not because they were incredible sprinters, but because one of the Jewish children had slipped on some ice and now sat on the cold ground, crying. Her Jewish friends huddled behind her, loyally sticking with her, though they all looked as if they'd rather run and hide. They were surrounded by the sneering bunch of older boys when Korinna and Rita came upon them.

"Jew, Jew, I spit on you!" the boys chanted, and

then they all spit on the group of youngsters in the
center.

"Jew, Jew, I spit on you!" Rita joined the taunting
jeer. Korinna watched, her mouth suddenly dry.

Finally, one of the boys grew tired of spitting,
so he picked up a ball of snow and threw it. It
landed squarely on the fallen girl's cheek. When the
snow fell away, Korinna could see that there had
been ice mixed in with the snow and that it had cut
the little girl's face. Blood oozed from the little
scrapes and mingled with the girl's tears and the
melted snow.

Rita reached down and scooped up a handful of snow, patting it into a firm ball. Others were doing the same. She offered the snowball to her friend.

"Throw it," Rita urged.

Korinna took the cold ball into her hand. It was heavy with ice. She looked at the group of children in the center of the crowd. They were Jews. They were the enemy, and for the Fatherland to thrive, all enemies had to be put down.

"For the Fatherland," Korinna said under her breath, and she let the missile fly. She had good aim. She hit the little girl in the shoulder. The girl gave a sharp cry and lifted a hand to ward off further blows. For the Fatherland, Korinna reminded herself firmly as she watched the tears continue to roll down the girl's face. For the Fatherland.

"Let's go," Korinna said, pulling on Rita's sleeve. Rita was still chanting. Korinna pulled harder. "Come on, we'll be late for dinner and our meeting."

Reluctantly, Rita allowed herself to be led away from the growing group of chanters.

It was quite a few blocks before Korinna couldn't hear the mocking refrain anymore, and still she couldn't get the little girl's expression out of her mind.

"I think we taught those dirty Jews a lesson," Rita said. "Did you see that girl's face when she was hit with that first snowball?" Rita giggled. "Maybe they'll stay where they belong instead of walking around like they have rights or something."

Korinna only nodded, and they walked on in silence. For the Fatherland, she kept telling herself. For the beloved Fatherland.

———————

Later, during the meeting, Fräulein Schönwald taught the girls the new song and they practiced it for the rest of the afternoon. At the end of the meeting all the girls formed a semicircle around the striking red, white, and black National Socialist flag, while one of the *Jungmädel* leaders regaled them with yet another story about their wonderful Führer. At the end of the lively speech everyone raised her right arm to a forty-five degree angle and shouted, *"Heil Hitler!"*

The sudden shout startled Korinna out of her thoughts. *"Heil Hitler,"* she said hastily, her voice trailing well behind the others.

"Korinna!" called an angry voice. "Come here!"

Korinna walked over to the leader, who stared furiously down her long nose.

"You have missed two meetings, Fräulein, and now you show your disrespect by failing to salute the flag properly!"

"But I—"

"Silence! You have not been told to speak!" commanded the leader.

"No, but—"

Suddenly a flash of heat stung her face as the leader slapped her hard across the cheek. The force of the blow jolted Korinna's head to the side. Immediately tears sprang into her eyes.

"I'll be watching you, Korinna Rehme," warned the leader tersely.

Korinna didn't wait to hear more. She turned and fled, grabbing her bag and coat on the way out of the silent room.

Chapter Eight

The cold air whipped against Korinna's damp cheeks as she ran home. No one had *ever* hit her before. She was stunned by what had happened, and she didn't want to think about it. She especially didn't want to talk about it when she got home, so she slowed her pace as she neared her house and carefully wiped the tears from her cheeks. She didn't want her mother asking any questions.

When she got home she found a note from her mother saying she was visiting with Frau Reineke, her mother's best friend. Glad no one was home, Korinna took off her coat and clumped up the stairs to her room. Leaving her book bag by the wardrobe as she always did, she lay down on her bed and stared at the ceiling.

Life was terrible, plain and simple, she thought. Her parents were traitors, and she hadn't done anything to remedy the situation. So she was a traitor, too. And now she had been slapped by her *Jungmädel* leader. Slapped hard!

She lifted a hand to her tender cheek as tears welled in her eyes again. She didn't understand why she had been attacked. What had she done wrong? So she had said, "*Heil Hitler*," a little out of unison—so what?

Korinna twisted over onto her stomach on her narrow bed, and buried her face in her pillow as tears began to flow in earnest. The *Jungmädel* was hers, it was where she belonged. Yet now she was suddenly punished in front of everyone, in front of all her friends and the other leaders, for something that seemed so inconsequential, so trivial.

Was she supposed to be exactly like everyone else? Move and speak at the same time? Dress exactly alike? Think and feel identically?

That's impossible, she thought, trying to hold back a sob that tightened her throat. Finally it erupted into the stillness of the room. Not only was it impossible, she didn't even *want* to be exactly like everyone else! Another sob escaped, and then another, and another, until each one sounded like an echo of the one before.

All the fear and anger Korinna had been holding inside these last few days gave vent through her tears. Nothing was fair. Nothing was right. Nothing! Neither her parents nor her *Jungmädel*—the two things she counted on the most—were the way they were supposed to be.

Finally her sobs quieted to join the stillness of the

house. Korinna held her breath to listen to the silence, and that's when she heard the soft meow of her kitten. She lifted her hot, tear-stained face from the pillow just in time to see the kitten come scrambling up onto her bed.

Korinna gathered the little bundle in her arms. "Hello, little one," she crooned, sitting up and rubbing her stuffy nose against the silken fur.

Suddenly, a thought struck her. She didn't know why she had thought she was alone when this whole time there had been two people not four meters away from her bed. She glanced suspiciously at the wardrobe, but it looked firmly in place against the wall. Where had her kitten come from? she wondered, still staring at the wardrobe. Someone had let the kitten out of the hiding room, she guessed, because she was almost sure the kitten hadn't been out before or it would have greeted her sooner.

She was embarrassed to think of the Jews listening to her crying. They had no right to eavesdrop on her, she thought angrily. But just as quickly her anger dissipated. For heaven's sake, she thought, exasperated with herself, what were the Krugmanns supposed to do? Knock on the wall and tell her they could hear every sob and that she was disturbing them?

A sudden giggle tried to escape, but it got lodged in her throat, swallowed back just in time. Hiding Jews in a back room was no laughing matter. Obviously, one of them had let the kitten out of the hiding room for a reason, and she had a strong suspicion the reason was to make her feel better. And it had worked, she realized with a slight smile.

Korinna stroked the head of her purring kitten, while still staring absently at the wardrobe. She didn't exactly like the idea of the Jews being considerate; after all, it was contrary to everything she had ever learned about this contemptible enemy.

Just then she heard the front door open. Her mother was home. Laying aside the kitten, she hurried into the bathroom to wash cold water over her heated face, trying to erase all trace of her tears.

"Korinna?" her mother called.

Korinna went downstairs and greeted her mother in the front hall with a hug.

Her mother stepped back from her daughter and frowned slightly. "Are you all right?"

"I'm fine. Why?"

Frau Rehme shrugged. "Your face looks red and you hugged me so hard, I thought you'd crush me."

Korinna grinned. "I'm just happy to see you. What are you making for supper?" she asked, following her mother into the kitchen.

"What do you think?" Frau Rehme said dryly. "Bread and cheese, bread and jam. Oh, and maybe a bit of butter here and there."

Korinna laughed. "Well, it's not too exciting, but you always manage to make everything taste good, Mother."

Her mother smiled. "You must have had a good day at school today." She tied an apron around her waist. "Did you have fun at your *Jungmädel* meeting after school?" she asked, glancing at her daughter.

"Yes," Korinna replied casually, avoiding her mother's eyes. "We learned a new song for the Führer's visit."

"Oh," was all her mother said in response. She changed the subject. "Here, peel these potatoes for tomorrow."

Korinna took the pile from her mother and sat down to peel off the dirty skins. Potatoes and more potatoes. Sometimes they got meat. Sometimes they got sugar. Sometimes they got butter. Times were hard, but they'd get better thanks to Adolf Hitler. *Wouldn't they?* Abruptly Korinna pushed that doubt out of her mind. Just because of a little slap she shouldn't be losing her faith in the Führer and in the Fatherland. Life would get better once enemies, such as the Krugmanns, were subdued.

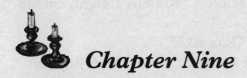 *Chapter Nine*

"Korinna, did you hear me?" Rita demanded as they walked to their *Jungmädel* meeting on Friday.

"What?"

Rita looked at her friend through narrowed eyes. "What's the matter with you today?"

"I'm sorry," Korinna said. "I feel a little light-headed. I must still be sick. In fact, I don't think I should stop at your house and then go to the meeting."

"I don't blame you, after what happened yesterday," Rita said.

Korinna almost thought she saw a smirk on her best friend's face. But she must have imagined it, she told herself quickly.

"That's not why," Korinna said defensively. "I'm just feeling a bit tired. You go on. Tomorrow you can tell me what happened." She started to turn down a side street toward her house.

"I don't think I'll go today, either," Rita said unexpectedly, turning the corner with her friend. "I'll come home with you. It's been so long since you've had me over after school, Korinna. And remember, your mother did invite me over this week."

"But that was before—" Korinna abruptly cut herself off.

"Before what?" Rita asked.

Korinna shook her head, "Never mind. But you can't come over anyway."

"Why not?"

"I . . . my mother isn't expecting you," Korinna stammered. "She won't have enough food prepared."

"That's fine. I won't stay for dinner. Your mother won't mind if I just stop by, will she?"

At one time, Korinna knew her mother wouldn't have minded. But now that the Jews had moved in. . . . She wondered what the Krugmanns were doing at that moment.

"You know I'm always welcome at your house," Rita persisted. "What's gotten into you?"

"What?"

"There you go again!" Rita exclaimed. "You're impossible!"

Korinna shook her head as though to clear it. "I'm sorry, Rita, I really must still be sick. Maybe it's better if you don't come over," she said, forcing herself to sound calm.

"I'll only come for a little while. Unless, of course,

you *really* don't want me to," Rita said in a casual voice.

Korinna sighed. They were almost to her house. "No, it's alright. You can come over, but not for too long. I think I should lie down for a bit before dinner."

"Fine. I won't stay long," Rita said as she preceded her friend to the front door and walked in without waiting for Korinna.

Korinna followed on her friend's heels. "Hello, Mother," she called as soon as she was in the house.

"Did you have to yell right in my ear?" Rita demanded, lifting a hand to her right ear. "This house isn't that big."

Korinna smiled wanly at her friend, then turned her attention to her mother who'd just stepped into the small front hall.

"Why, hello, Rita," Frau Rehme said politely. "I haven't seen you here lately. You should stop by more often."

Rita turned her head slightly and grinned at Korinna. Korinna didn't bother smiling back.

"Thank you, Frau Rehme. Korinna and I decided to skip our meeting this afternoon. We thought it was best after what happened at yesterday's meeting."

"Oh? What happened?" asked Korinna's mother with a raised eyebrow.

Rita's eyes flew wide. "You mean Korinna didn't tell you the awful thing that happened?"

"No, she didn't," Frau Rehme said. "But I'm sure you will," she added wryly.

Korinna poked her finger into her friend's back. "It was nothing. Come on, let's go upstairs."

"But, Korinna, you really should tell your mother what happened yesterday. I'm sure she wants to know." Rita turned to Frau Rehme. "Korinna was slapped by one of our leaders for not saluting the flag properly!"

"Oh, is that all?" Korinna's mother turned to her daughter. "You really should do things properly, dear, or you'll be punished. It's only right that your leader slapped you. You must learn to be more respectful."

Korinna lowered her gaze. She couldn't believe her mother was responding like this. She hadn't wanted to tell her about the slap yesterday because she hadn't wanted her to get upset. But her mother wasn't upset. Korinna felt a lump form in her throat.

"Korinna?" her mother said gently.

Korinna looked up. Her mother's eyes shone with tears. She *was* upset! It suddenly dawned on Korinna that her mother just didn't want Rita to know. She smiled tremulously at her mother.

"You're right, Mother," she said evenly. "I was just tired from not feeling well these last few days. It won't happen again. I promise."

"I should hope not," Frau Rehme said firmly.

"Let's go upstairs," Korinna said to her friend. "Or maybe we should just sit in here," she amended quickly, pointing to the front room. She didn't want to chance Rita hearing any "mouse noises" from behind her wardrobe.

Rita shook her head. "No, let's go up to your room."

Korinna reluctantly led her friend up the stairs.

In Korinna's room, Rita said, "I thought your mother would get upset about the slap."

"Then why did you tell her?" Korinna asked loudly as she purposely dumped her book bag noisily against the wardrobe. She hoped the Krugmanns could hear her talking to Rita and would keep quiet.

"I just thought she ought to know. You are her daughter, after all," Rita said defensively.

"Next time let me do the telling," Korinna said, unable to keep the anger from her voice.

"Sorry."

Korinna glanced at her friend. She didn't look sorry. "Oh, forget it."

"Where's your kitten?" Rita asked.

Korinna froze. She'd forgotten about the kitten. Where was she? With Rachel?

"Here, kitty," Rita called, leaning down and looking under Korinna's desk.

"No. Don't do that," Korinna said quickly, fearing she'd hear a soft meow coming from behind the wardrobe. "She doesn't answer to that. She'll come out when she feels like it."

Rita frowned. "Where does she hide? Can we go look for her?"

Korinna tried to sound enthusiastic. "Sure, let's try downstairs. She loves the kitchen." She knew they probably wouldn't find the kitten anywhere except behind her wardrobe, but at least she was getting Rita out of her room and away from the Krugmann's hideaway.

The girls found Korinna's mother in the kitchen. "Mother," Korinna said. "Have you seen my kitten?"

"No, I haven't, dear. But let me help you look. I'll search upstairs," Frau Rehme said quickly, hurrying out of the room.

"Haven't you named your kitten yet?" Rita asked.

"Not yet. I can't think of a good name," Korinna said, making a show of looking for her kitten behind the stove.

Rita stooped to look under the kitchen chairs.

"Here she is," Frau Rehme called from the top landing.

Korinna followed her friend up the stairs.

"So she was up here after all," Rita said, taking the kitten from Frau Rehme's hands.

"Thank you, Mother."

Korinna's mother squeezed one of her daughter's hands as they passed each other on the stairs.

"She's cute," Rita said begrudgingly, tickling the kitten on the stomach. The kitten kicked and clawed with her sharp nails. "Ouch!" Rita exclaimed. She yanked her hand away from the kitten's grip. "She tried to bite me."

Korinna smiled, taking the animal from Rita.

"She's just playing." She scratched her pet behind the ears.

Rita moved to sit on the edge of the bed, as Korinna continued to stroke the kitten.

"My parents are the enemy," Rita read out loud.

Korinna's head jerked up. Her hand reached forward to grab the black notebook from Rita's hands, but she wasn't quick enough. She had left the book under her pillow.

"What does this mean?" Rita asked, standing on the bed to hold the book above Korinna's reaching hand.

Korinna's heart leapt to her throat. "Nothing. It means nothing. I was just mad at my parents one day. I don't even remember why."

Rita jumped off the bed and hid the black book back under Korinna's pillow. "Better watch what you write," she warned. "If a *Jungmädel* leader read that, she'd ask you a lot of questions. Of course I believe what you just told me, but a leader might not." Rita's eyes darted around the room. Was it Korinna's imagination, or did her friends eyes rest a little longer on the wardrobe than on anything else?

Korinna was glad when Rita said she had to go home.

"Don't tell anyone about what I wrote," Korinna said. She wasn't ready to turn in her parents yet.

Rita paused in the doorway. "I won't. Your secret's safe with me." Then she raced down the stairs and out the front door.

When she was sure Rita was gone, Korinna tore the page out of her black notebook and put the book in her bag. She took the page and ripped it into tiny pieces, trying not to think about what she was doing.

After dinner, Korinna sat down at her desk and tried to do her homework. She wrote a short essay and studied her history book, but it was hard to concentrate for some reason. Finally she gave up. Looking out the window, the murky sky depressed her. She closed the drapes to shut out the gloom, but it didn't help. The gloom had settled in her heart.

On sudden impulse, she knocked on the wardrobe, then slowly pulled it away from the wall. The candlelight from the hidden room spilled out into her bedroom. Sophie, pale, eyes wide, stared up at Korinna. No one spoke for a full minute. Korinna didn't know what to say. What was she doing?

She caught Rachel's gaze. The little girl's eyes were dark and wide like her mother's, but while the mother's held fear and suspicion, Rachel's eyes looked sad and lonely.

Still Korinna couldn't speak. She motioned for the little girl to crawl out of her cramped space into Korinna's room. Rachel asked her mother with her eyes, and after a slight pause, Sophie gave a curt nod. Rachel scrambled out from behind the wardrobe, and Korinna pushed it back into place.

Korinna and Rachel sat in the darkening room, facing each other, legs crossed, elbows on knees.

"Do you want to play?" Rachel whispered.

Korinna shrugged. "Play what?"

"We could play dress up, or house," Rachel said, her excited voice soon rising above a whisper. "You could be the daddy and I'm the mommy. Or let's play soldier."

"Soldier?" Korinna said.

"You're a soldier and I'm a Jew and you capture me; then we switch places and you're the Jew."

"Why would you want to play that?" Korinna asked sharply.

"I've never played it before," Rachel said, her voice dropping as though she sensed she'd said something she shouldn't have.

"Then how do you know about this . . . this game?"

"The boys who lived nearby used to play it."

"What boys?"

"Hendrik and Werner, and some of the other boys."

"Were they Jews?"

Rachel's eyes widened. "No," she whispered.

Korinna shook her head. She didn't understand the heat she felt inside. She didn't understand her sudden longing to take little Rachel on her lap and sing to her. She didn't understand anything anymore.

At that moment, her mother walked into the bedroom. She pulled aside the wardrobe and said, "The sun has set. I thought you'd like to know."

"Thank you," Frau Krugmann said, laying aside her sewing.

Puzzled, Korinna watched Rachel crawl back behind the wardrobe.

"It's time for the Krugmann's Sabbath prayers," Frau Rehme said, as though sensing Korinna's question.

She looked to say good-bye to Rachel, but what Frau Krugmann was doing caught her eye instead. She had turned a box upside down and on it she had placed two candlesticks. Visions of a similar scene popped into her head, and she recalled her childhood friend Anita inviting her over for the Sabbath prayers and dinner a few times. It had been so long ago she'd forgotten. But now a strange yearning for her childhood washed over her. How simple it had been then, with Anita Scheinman as her best friend, and nothing more to worry about than whether her dolls had enough to eat, and if Papa would tell her a story after supper.

The Krugmanns now stared at the candles, waiting to be left alone. Quietly Korinna pushed the wardrobe against the wall, shutting out the soft sound of the melodic Hebrew prayers.

Chapter Ten

Korinna aimed the snowball carefully. Then, in one fluid motion, she let the missile fly from her hand, directly at Rachel's face. But when the snowball hit its target, it turned out to be a glass ball instead of one made of snow, and it shattered into a million brilliant shards, each one piercing Rachel's skin. And Rachel just stared at her attacker with wide, innocent eyes filled with tears. Then came the banging. A loud solid banging, sounding as if God were knocking on the steel colored clouds, demanding to be let down to earth.

Korinna woke up, but the banging continued. It wasn't God knocking from above, it was someone pounding on the front door below. She heard her father walking down the stairs.

Korinna's mother came into her room. "Are you awake?" she whispered through the darkness.

"Yes, Mother. What's going on? Who's at the door?" Korinna asked as the banging continued.

"It must be the Gestapo," Frau Rehme said, her voice trembling with anxiety. "No one else would come in the middle of the night."

Korinna's heart shuddered in her chest. "The Gestapo! But why? Will they find the Krugmanns?" She sat up, her hands clenched tightly on her blankets.

"Hush, there's no time for questions now," her mother said as she softly knocked a rhythmic beat against Korinna's wall. She stopped, and then repeated the prearranged warning once again.

"Pretend you are sleeping," she told her daughter, and she quickly left the room as they heard the front door open and the booted officers stomp into the small front hall.

"What's going on?" Korinna heard her father demand.

"This is a search," said one of the officers in a brusque voice. "There are some stinking Jews hiding in this area, and we just want to make sure they're not here."

"We are loyal Germans, loyal to the Führer," Herr Rehme protested, glancing at the Führer's picture.

"It's easy to hang a picture," said a second man.

Korinna recognized Hans's voice. Did Rita know her brother was searching her best friend's house? Maybe Rita herself had told him about her black notebook. But no, Rita wouldn't do that. She was her best friend. And she'd promised she wouldn't tell anyone.

Korinna could hear banging and stomping downstairs. Soon the noise made its way upstairs.

"Go in there," Hans said to her parents. She heard them move into their own room. When her door swung open she closed her eyes tightly, and she heard the heavy hammering of her heart pounding in her ears. She saw the bright stab of light behind her eyelids as someone aimed a flashlight at her from her doorway. Then the light moved away.

Korinna watched through slitted eyes as Hans walked into her room and looked under her bed. He walked over to her closet. She held her breath. He opened and shut each drawer with a snap. Then he opened the cupboard-like doors behind which she hung her blouses and skirts. Pushing aside the clothes, he felt the back of the wardrobe. Korinna was sure Hans must be able to hear the frantic pounding of her heart and her erratic breathing. Finally, Rita's brother closed the wardrobe doors with a bang and stalked out of the room, a frown pulling at his face. He looked as if he were disappointed at not finding anything.

Korinna didn't dare move until she was positive she was really alone in her room. Then she tried to relax her rigid body and her clenched fists, but she couldn't. She listened to the men search the bathroom and then move into her parents' bedroom.

She heard only the swish and snap of drawers

being opened and closed. Suddenly her father's voice rang out. "Leave those alone!"

"Bernd, no," her mother cried.

Something heavy fell against her parents' desk. Terrified, she scrambled out of bed and raced into her parents' bedroom.

Everyone turned to look at Korinna as she ran into the room. She stopped abruptly, her heart pounding, as she took in the scene before her.

Her father was sprawled on the floor, partially raised up against the foot of the desk. A narrow line of blood, trickling from his nose, shone in the bright overhead light. Her mother crouched protectively beside him, and Hans stood menacingly over the two of them, holding the brass figurine in his fist, ready to strike again.

"No!" Korinna cried, immediately running to her father's side, tears stinging her eyes. "What have you done?" she demanded, looking up at Hans's face.

"Go back to bed," her father commanded, struggling to stand up.

His wife took his arm to help support him. "Be careful, Bernd."

Hans looked as if he would step forward to hit Herr Rehme again.

"No, Hans!" Korinna said, standing up and suddenly moving forward to hold back the officer's arm. "Leave them alone! Please!" she begged.

Hans shook his arm free and looked down at Korinna with a scowl. Korinna remembered playing

tag with Hans when he had been young. She even remembered having a crush on him at one time, giggling and following him around like a puppy. It seemed like so long ago. Did he remember?

Slowly he lowered his arm and tossed away the figurine. It thudded onto the floor. "Come," he said to his fellow Gestapo officer. Then he took another sweeping look around the room before turning sharply on his booted heel and marching out of the room.

The Rehmes didn't speak as they listened to the two men stomp down the stairs and finally out the front door, leaving it gaping open behind them. They heard the car roar to life, then drive off. Apparently they were through searching the neighborhood for the night.

Not until the sound of the car was swallowed up in the quiet of the night did Korinna dare breathe again. Then all the tension left her, and her knees started to quiver.

Now her father sat on the edge of his bed, his red hair an unruly mass around his head, holding a white cloth to his nose. Korinna's mother came over to her daughter and hugged her, rocking her back and forth.

"It's over now, dear," she crooned.

Korinna sniffed back her tears. "What happened? Why did Hans hit Papa?"

"They were searching through my drawer with the photographs in it. Papa worried they would ruin them with their rough hands. See? They ripped that one there," she said, nodding toward a precious photograph of Korinna's grandfather, which now lay on the floor, practically in two pieces.

"Damned Nazis!" growled Korinna's father. "Insanity," he said. "That's what it is. Insanity." He turned to his daughter. "Are you all right, Korinna?"

She nodded.

"It was very brave of you to step forward like that, but also very stupid. Next time stay in your room," he ordered.

Korinna felt the sting of the reprimand. "But I know Hans. *You* know Hans. He shouldn't have been treating you like that."

"We knew the *old* Hans, Korinna. Things have changed. People have changed. It's too dangerous to intercept the Gestapo. They don't listen to reason, Korinna."

"Now go to bed," her mother said gently.

Korinna slowly walked back into her own room and got into bed. She wasn't too anxious to rejoin the dream of throwing the ball of glass at Rachel, but she closed her eyes anyway. She blew into her icy hands, trying to warm them. They still trembled.

A few weeks ago she never would have believed she could be as frightened as she was right now. Hadn't she recently told her mother she had nothing to fear from anyone because she was a loyal German? And now, what? Now she was a traitor and it seemed she feared almost everyone. Suddenly no one could be trusted. Should she trust Rita, her best friend? Or should she trust the Krugmanns, the hated enemy?

And who did she love? Of course she loved her

parents, but they were traitors to the Fatherland. And she had always loved her Führer, but now his officers were frightening her. Nothing made any sense anymore.

Chapter Eleven

Korinna didn't see the Krugmanns again except at meal times when she helped her mother deliver food and later take away the dirty dishes.

Sunday afternoon, Korinna felt restless. It was hard to imagine little Rachel cooped up behind her bedroom wall, day after day after day. She was bored, yet she could go anywhere. Rachel must be going crazy, Korinna decided.

On sudden impulse, she knocked on the wardrobe and then pulled it away from the wall. Two faces peered anxiously up at her. Because it was daylight out, it would be too dangerous for Rachel to come out into her room with the curtains open. And it would be too suspicious looking to close the curtains this early in the day, so Korinna knew if she wanted to keep Rachel company, she would have to venture into the dark, smelly hole the Krugmanns had been forced to call a home for the past week.

Without giving herself a chance to think and thereby change her mind, she grabbed a few sheets of paper and, taking one last deep breath of fresh air, squatted down and crawled into the narrow space between the walls.

She knew she wouldn't suffocate in the small room because air holes had been drilled into the bathroom. But the space was so confining, Korinna still felt short of breath. Pulling the wardrobe almost closed, she couldn't help smiling to hear Rachel's excited chatter.

"You've never been in here before," Rachel said, sounding pleased to have a visitor. "Mama sleeps there," she said, pointing to a pile of old blankets which Korinna supposed served as a mattress. "And I sleep here, next to my baby."

Korinna looked in the empty, makeshift cradle. "What's that?" she asked, pointing to some rough hewn boards propped against the narrow wall behind Frau Krugmann's sleeping space.

Rachel giggled. "That's the bathroom."

"Oh."

The room was narrow, fitting somehow between her bedroom and the bathroom, and also between the hall and the outside wall of the house. The space would have been impossibly small if it hadn't been for the closet in the bathroom which had a fake back to it. Towels were placed in the closet to make it appear deeper than it was, but in fact, it was shallow to allow more room behind it in the hidden room. The other night her father had explained that no one would ever guess the room was hidden there, unless they were specifically and carefully looking for it. And that would never happen, her father had promised.

"What's this?" Rachel asked, lifting the paper and finding the small box Korinna had brought in with the sheets of paper.

Korinna smiled. "What does it look like?"

Rachel opened the box carefully. Out spilled a number of pencils of different colors. "They're beautiful," the little girl breathed reverently. She looked up at Korinna. "Are they for me to use?"

"They're for you to keep!" Korinna said. She had found them in a box under her bed when she had recently been looking for the kitten.

"To keep? Honestly?" the girl asked, her eyes wide with disbelief.

"Of course. Why would I lie to you?"

"Because you don't like Jews," Rachel said simply.

Korinna swallowed uneasily, afraid to look up to see if Sophie listened to their conversation.

She stared down at Rachel's bent head, searching for some reply. Could she deny it? Could she defend it? What should she say?

"I like this color best," Rachel said, holding up a pencil.

Startled out of her thoughts, Korinna said, "What?"

"This is my favorite color," Rachel repeated.

But what about what you just said? Korinna wanted to ask. I'm supposed to hate Jews, yet here I am giving my colored pencils to you. I should get up and leave, she thought. But instead, she said, "Why is that your favorite color?"

"It's the color of the setting sun and the color of your hair."

Korinna picked up a pencil of burnt umber. "And this is the color of your hair."

Rachel's smile disappeared. "I wish my hair were this color," she said, fondling the reddish yellow pencil.

"Why?"

Rachel twirled the pencil between her fingers. "Then I wouldn't have to hide. If I had light hair, no one would know I was Jewish and I wouldn't have to stay in this horrible little room!"

"Rachel!" Sophie said sharply. "You're lucky to have a room like this. Just think of poor Papa and Ruthie who have to sleep with cows and goats."

Rachel's lips turned down at the corners. "I want Ruth and Papa to be here," she wailed.

"Shhhh," Sophie said.

The little girl bent her head and cried against her lifted knees.

Korinna looked back and forth between Sophie and Rachel. All the pity she had been working so hard to keep from feeling now pinched at her heart. She picked up a sheet of paper and began to draw. After a few moments, Rachel's sobs quieted to an occasional hiccup. Finally, she lifted her head and watched Korinna draw.

"What's that?" Rachel asked.

"This," Korinna said, putting the finishing touches on the flower boxes, "is your house."

Rachel frowned. "No, it's not. My house doesn't look like that. My house has white shutters and it's bigger."

"Well, this is the house where you live now. This is what it looks like in the summer. Now there are no flowers in the window boxes, and there are long thick icicles hanging from the roof."

Understanding began to show on Rachel's face. "You mean this is *this* house? This is where we are right now?"

Korinna nodded.

Rachel smiled. "I like this house," she said. "It's pretty, even if it is smaller than mine. I like it very much." She nodded her head and took the drawing from Korinna, placing it next to her mattress. "Now I know where I am," she said happily, and she picked up the yellow pencil and started drawing on a clean sheet of paper while Korinna watched.

Later, a knock on the wall startled Korinna. As the wardrobe pulled away from the opening, her heart beat faster. Even after she saw that it was just her mother with the midday dinner, her palms stayed sweaty and the heat around her neck still choked her. She wondered if the same thing happened to the Krugmanns every time the wardrobe moved. She glanced over at Sophie and saw that the older woman looked tense, staring at the opening with wide eyes.

Korinna hastily looked away, feeling as if she were spying.

Korinna crawled out from behind the wardrobe so the Krugmanns could eat. Before she closed the wardrobe, she opened her bottom desk drawer and pulled out a doll. The doll had a China face and hands, but the nose was chipped and a couple of fingers on the right hand were missing. And the doll had been so tightly hugged that it was rather limp through the middle.

Korinna held out the doll to Rachel. "Here."

"She's beautiful," Rachel said breathlessly, not yet lifting her hands to take it, as though afraid it would be snatched away at the last moment.

"She's for you."

Reverently, Rachel took the doll. Briefly, their hands touched. Korinna smiled as the little girl carefully cradled the doll in her arms. "*Tag* never lies still in the cradle for me," Rachel said, her eyes not leaving the doll's blushed cheeks.

"*Tag?*" Korinna asked.

"The kitten," Sophie explained. "Rachel only sees the kitten in the day when you're not home. So she named it *Tag*—Day."

Korinna smiled. "I like that name. I have to admit, I never got around to naming the kitten myself. *Tag* is the perfect name."

Rachel lifted her eyes once again. "I like my doll," she said. "And I like you. You're so nice."

Korinna swallowed hard. Didn't the girl realize

they were enemies? She was a loyal German, and Rachel was a Jew. Like oil and water, they just didn't mix. They could not be friends.

On Monday, Korinna didn't get a chance to talk to Rita until they met after dinner on their way to the *Jungmädel* meeting.

"Why aren't you wearing your uniform?" Rita demanded upon seeing Korinna in a sweater and gray skirt.

"It was dirty."

Rita frowned. "How do you expect to get back on the good side out the leaders if you don't even wear the uniform?"

"I only have one," Korinna said. "Mother's washing it for me today so I can wear it tomorrow. At least I'm wearing my kerchief," she said.

Rita shrugged. "If you had two uniforms you wouldn't run into this problem."

"My family can't afford another uniform," Korinna said evenly, trying to keep her anger in check. "And you know that, Rita."

"Maybe if your mother participated more in the Nazi Women's Organization, someone would offer to help you."

Korinna stopped walking and faced her friend. "Are you trying to say that my mother isn't a good German?" she demanded.

"I'm just saying that she isn't the most loyal person in this town."

"My mother loves Germany! She—she's just as loyal as your mother. She's just too busy to go regularly to the Women's Organization."

"Busy doing what?" Rita asked.

"Guten Tag!" Eva called, walking up to the two girls.

"Hello," Korinna said tersely.

Rita ignored the other girl.

"What's going on with you two?" Eva said, stepping around the girls to continue on her way. "Aren't you coming to the meeting?" she asked when she didn't get an answer.

"Yes," Korinna said quickly. "We're coming." She walked beside Eva, leaving Rita glaring after them.

"What was that all about?" Eva asked under her breath.

"Nothing," Korinna said. She was glad Eva had interrupted her conversation with Rita. She didn't think Rita could really be suspicious of her mother, but she didn't want to be questioned anyway.

They walked a few moments in silence.

"I'm sorry, Korinna," Rita said, who was walking behind the other two girls.

Korinna didn't stop walking or even turn around.

"I mean it, Korinna. You're my best friend, and I know your mother is a loyal German. I didn't mean to sound so suspicious or anything."

Now Korinna stopped and turned around. "I know," she said. "I shouldn't have been so defensive."

"Are we still friends?" Rita asked.

Korinna opened her arms wide. "Of course." The two girls hugged each other while Eva watched.

"You'll always be my best friend," Rita said.

Korinna grinned. "You, too."

"Now that that's settled, can we go?" Eva asked dryly.

Korinna and Rita smiled at each other and started walking arm in arm, which forced Eva to walk behind them. But Korinna didn't want the other girl to feel left out, so she pushed Rita to the edge of the sidewalk and pulled Eva up to walk beside them. On the rest of the way to the meeting they sang their favorite song, "Now Is the Time."

Now is the time
The hour calls to action
To cut down evil
To bring about a new world

Where every man on earth will have a good life
*   and home.*

On the horizon we see a bright light.
The earth is turning to a new and better
*   future.*
As false gods fall
All men will be free . . .

As they reached the building where their meetings were held, their voices trailed off.

Korinna took a deep breath. The last time she'd been to a meeting, she'd been slapped. Today she would be sure to do everything right. She didn't want to be humiliated in front of everyone again.

The Troop meeting passed without a problem. Korinna paid close attention to everything, not letting her mind wander for an instant. The leaders acted as if nothing had happened. They even commended her on carrying extra pamphlets in her book bag because they needed them to give to a new member. Rita collected them from Korinna's book bag along with some of the other girls'.

Eva had to leave the meeting early to take care of her younger brother, so Korinna and Rita walked home together after the meeting. The bright sky was already fading to darkness, and a cold wind whipped at the girls as they buried their chins in their scarves.

"What?" Korinna said at hearing Rita mumble something.

"I forgot to ask you if you'd heard about the Reinekes," Rita repeated, this time lifting her face to the wind.

Korinna looked obliquely at her friend, not wanting to lift the lower portion of her face from the warmth of her scarf. She shook her head, but Rita wasn't looking at her, so she had to lift her head a bit and say, "No, what happened to them?"

"Hans searched their house last night."

Visions of the search on her own house raced through her head. She wondered if Rita knew that Hans had hit her father. "So?" she said.

"He found something there," Rita said.

Korinna could hear the suppressed excitement in the other girl's voice. "What did he find?"

"Jews!"

"Jews?" Korinna felt a sudden painful tightness in her stomach. "Jews?" she repeated.

"Two of them. They were hiding in the pantry. Hans said he sniffed them out, they stank so bad," Rita said gleefully.

"How do you know all this?"

"Hans came over this morning before I went to school. He was up all night searching houses."

"Who were the Jews?" Korinna asked.

"Who cares who they were?" Rita said. "They're Jews, that's all anyone needs to know. I think they were a husband and wife."

"What's going to happen to the Reinekes?" Korinna asked, hoping she sounded casual.

"The Reinekes have been arrested. Hans said they'll probably be sent to a work camp, if they're not shot first."

The knot in Korinna's stomach pulled even tighter at this news. "What about the Jews?" Korinna asked, trying not to sound too interested.

"Who cares what happens to the Jews?" Rita said derisively. "They'll be sent away somewhere. Hans told Papa they were trying to leave Germany because they didn't want to be arrested or be sent to a work camp. Imagine," she said, shaking her head, "Jews still think they have the right to make choices. The sooner they're all rounded up and sent away, the better it will be for all of us loyal Germans."

Korinna nodded briefly in agreement.

"I can't believe that some of them are still in town. Not that it does them any good with their synagogues closed and their shops closed. I'd think they'd all *want* to go live somewhere else with other Jews. At least they'd be with their own kind."

"Isn't Frau Reineke your mother's best friend?" Rita continued, once more burying her chin in her neck scarf.

"I suppose they're friendly. Or at least they were," Korinna said. She knew that wasn't exactly the truth. The truth was that they had been the best of friends since they were children, and they still were.

"Well, I certainly hope Frau Reineke's bad habits didn't rub off on your mother. Not that I think your mother is anything less than an absolutely loyal German," Rita added quickly.

"They haven't seen each other lately," Korinna lied.

Rita nodded. "That's good, because any friends of the Reinekes will probably be under suspicion now. At least that's what my brother told Papa."

"Did Hans also tell him that he searched our

house?" Korinna asked bitterly before she could stop herself. "And that he hit my father? Hans knocked him on the floor."

Rita looked startled, and she shook her head. "No, Korinna, I swear, he didn't say anything about that. What happened?"

"He was ruining some of my mother's photographs and my father told him to be careful. Hans hit my father and made him bleed."

"I didn't know that, Korinna. Honest, I didn't."

Korinna shrugged as if she didn't care, carefully taking control of her anger. "Hans was just doing his job. Papa shouldn't have interfered," she said, trying to sound nonchalant.

Rita nodded. "That's true, but still, I'm surprised Hans hit your father. Hans is usually so gentle."

Korinna suppressed a shudder. Visions of Hans kicking Herr Haase the other day popped into her mind. And the Hans she had seen the night he'd searched their house had been far from gentle.

Korinna turned down her path. "I'll see you tomorrow." She waved to Rita and then stepped into the warmth of her house.

As she took off her coat and boots, she realized her hands were trembling.

She found her mother in the front room. She was sitting in the dark with the curtains wide open.

"Mother?" Korinna said softly, sitting down beside her on the couch. She could see the sheen of tears on her mother's cheeks. "Mother, what's wrong?"

"Frau Reineke," was all she said, reminding Korinna what Rita had told her. Her mother's best friend had been arrested for harboring Jews. Would her parents be next? she wondered as she took her mother's cold hands into her own trembling ones.

Suddenly her mother let out a sob, which sounded like it was wrenched from the bottom of her soul. The sound ripped through the quiet of the room and squeezed Korinna's heart. Frau Rehme put her arms around her daughter and cried against Korinna's shoulder. Korinna pulled her mother close, feeling helpless, yet somehow in charge.

Her mother had always been there to dry *her* tears. That's what mothers were for. But now she consoled her mother, murmuring under her breath and rocking her back and forth. She suddenly felt grown up, something she'd longed to be for quite some time. Only now she wasn't sure she liked the feeling, or the heavy sense of responsibility that came with it.

Herr Rehme finally came home, later than usual. He joined his family in the dark front room, enveloping his wife and daughter in his long, strong arms. No one said anything for quite a while. Finally Korinna's mother said, "The Krugmanns are probably hungry."

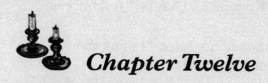

Chapter Twelve

It wasn't until the last few minutes of the *Jungmädel* meeting, after school the next day, that Korinna and Rita had a chance to talk.

Korinna eyed her friend nervously for a few moments, then she took a deep breath and said, "Rita, do you remember Anita Scheinmann?"

"That scrawny Jew?"

"That's right. The skinny little thing who used to live next door to me. Do you ever wonder what's happened to her?"

Rita glanced up from her tassel. "Every once in a while. Why?"

"Well, I wonder, too. I mean what's happened to all the Jews who used to live around here?"

"They've been sent east to live with other Jews. They're happier there with their own kind."

"Do you really think they're happier?"

"Of course they are."

Korinna nodded in agreement and didn't say anything.

Finally Rita broke the silence between them. "Do you think about the Jews a lot?"

"Not a lot," Korinna said hastily. "Just once in a while."

"Oh." Rita lowered her voice. "I think about them more than just once in awhile."

Korinna raised her gaze from her tassel and stared into Rita's blue eyes. "Really?" she said.

"Sure. I almost feel sorry for them."

"You do?" For a moment Korinna felt a wave of suspicion wash over her. Was this some kind of a trap? she wondered. She looked around the room, but no one was taking any notice of them. She looked back at Rita, but her friend was intent upon her project. Korinna felt ashamed of herself for suspecting Rita. Rita was her very best friend. It wasn't Rita who was lying and keeping secrets, it was Korinna. She was the one not acting like a best friend.

"I feel sorry for them, too," Korinna whispered under her breath.

"I thought you hated Jews," Rita said, also keeping her voice down.

"I did until—well, until a little while ago." As much as she trusted Rita, she just couldn't bring herself to tell her about the Krugmanns. Not yet.

"I don't really hate them," Rita said. "I just pretend so people think I do."

"I always believed you," Korinna said. "You should be an actress some day."

"I'd rather be a nurse. Hans told me they need nurses at the work camps to help the doctors who care for the Jews."

The camps couldn't be all that bad if they had doctors and nurses attending to the Jews, thought Korinna. But somehow it didn't make sense to her to lock up the Jews in work camps, and then give them medical care. She couldn't help wondering how much "care" they actually got.

"By the way," Korinna said, "have you seen my black book?"

Rita raise her pale blond eyebrows. "No, why?"

"I can't find it and I know I had it yesterday. I probably left it at home. It's just that—"

"Let's go," Rita said, interrupting her friend. The leaders were calling all the girls together.

"Wait for me after the meeting," Korinna said, twisting the extra twine into a ball.

"Oh, I can't," Rita said hastily.

"Why not?"

"I have to run an errand for my mother. You go on without me, and I'll see you tomorrow."

Korinna nodded slowly. "Okay," she said, trying to shrug away the uneasy feeling that suddenly settled on her shoulders like a heavy, itchy wool sweater. "I'll see you tomorrow."

As soon as Korinna walked in the door her mother called to her from the kitchen.

"What is it, Mother?" she said when she saw the drawn look on her mother's face.

"Sit down, Korinna," Frau Rehme said.

Korinna sat down at the table where her mother was peeling and cutting carrots. Cut onions were also on the table, no doubt accounting for the teary look in her mother's eyes.

"I've told you about Herr Krugmann and Ruth, Sophie's husband and fourteen-year-old daughter?"

"Yes, Mother, you've mentioned them. Rachel

130

talks about Ruth all the time. What's happened? Is something wrong?"

"It's Ruth," her mother said slowly. "She had pneumonia for weeks, but nothing could be done. She died last night."

Korinna sat in stunned silence. All she could imagine was Rachel's face when she heard the news. "Do Frau Krugmann and Rachel know?"

Korinna's mother nodded. "I told them as soon as I heard."

"Why couldn't they call a doctor?"

"There was no doctor in the area who could be trusted," Frau Rehme said sadly. "They did what they could for her, but living above a barn where it was cold and damp was the worst thing for her."

"Why didn't they move her?" Korinna demanded. She couldn't rid herself of the image of Rachel proudly bragging about her older sister. She must be devastated.

"The family that was hiding her couldn't move her. There was no safe place to go at the time," explained her mother. She got up from the table and came around to hug her daughter. "I'm so lucky to have you, *Liebling,*" she said softly.

Korinna felt her throat tighten. "Can I go see Rachel?"

Frau Rehme hesitated. "You can try. I don't know if she'll see you, though."

Korinna nodded and went upstairs. In her room, she quietly deposited her book bag by the wardrobe and then pulled the curtain over her window closed. She didn't care if it looked suspicious, she thought with a sudden flare of anger. It wasn't fair that she had to sneak around and try to act normal when every-thing was so—so mixed-up!

She knocked on the wall. Slowly she opened up the wardrobe and looked into the dimly lit room.

"Hello, Frau Krugmann," she said softly, crouch-ing down before the woman. For a moment they just stared at each other in silence. "Can Rachel come out for awhile?"

Sophie looked sadly at her daughter, who was curled up on the small mattress she used as a bed at night and play area during the day. "Rachel, do you want to play with Korinna?"

Rachel shook her head.

"Come out and draw with me," Korinna said.

"I never want to draw again," Rachel said in a trembling voice.

"Then just come out and sit with me," Korinna coaxed. "I don't feel very happy and I need someone to keep me company."

Rachel lifted her tear-stained face. Slowly she crawled over to the opening, and Korinna smiled at her encouragingly.

Korinna pulled away from the back room, leaving space for Rachel to come out. Then she pushed the *Schrank* back against the wall and focused on the little girl sitting cross-legged on the floor in front of her. She looked so small, so fragile. So innocent.

"Why are you staring at me?" Rachel asked in a small, tremulous voice.

"I was just wondering if you look like Ruth," Korinna said softly.

"Ruth is dead!" Rachel cried.

Korinna waved her hands through the air. "I know she's dead out here. But in here," she pointed to Rachel's heart, "she'll live as long as you do. As long as you remember her, and think of her, and love her."

Rachel eyed her suspiciously. "But I'll never see her again."

"But in a way you can see her whenever you want. Just close your eyes and think of her, and she'll be there."

A small hopeful look came over the little girl's face.

"Do you remember what Ruth looked like?" Korinna asked, reaching for some paper and some colored pencils she kept in a drawer in her desk.

Rachel nodded solemnly.

"Then why don't you draw her picture so you'll never forget. Then, in ten years from now, you can look at these pictures and remind yourself what Ruth looked like."

Rachel hesitantly took the paper and pencils. Then, with increasing determination she started to draw.

Korinna smiled at the girl and lifted one of her schoolbooks from her book bag. She opened the heavy volume and began to read while Rachel drew picture after picture of her sister Ruth.

When Frau Rehme came up with supper for the Krugmanns, Korinna took the pile of drawings from Rachel and began to look through them.

"This is Ruth playing the piano," Rachel said seriously. "She was the best in the whole world. And this is Ruth at home, lying on her bed. She did that a lot when she wasn't playing the piano."

One by one, Rachel explained each drawing. Korinna smiled and nodded at the appropriate moments, though the smile felt awkward. The little girl didn't seem to notice.

"You can keep this one with the others I gave you," Rachel said, handing Korinna a drawing.

"Thank you very much," Korinna said. "Now I think it's time for you to eat."

She opened the wardrobe and passed in the food her mother had left for the Krugmann's supper. She left the wardrobe ajar to let fresh air into the closed up space, and she put Rachel's drawing on her desk. It was a drawing of Ruth, holding a bouquet of multicolored flowers, staring out of the paper. Korinna's heart jumped, as it had when she'd been looking through Rachel's many drawings. In this one, as in all the others, Ruth's hair was sunshine yellow, not dark as it should have been. And her eyes were light blue instead of brown. She looked like Korinna, and Korinna realized sadly that Rachel had already forgotten what her older sister had looked like.

Chapter Thirteen

Later that night, much later, Korinna heard the soft tread of feet coming up the stairs. And though she had been warned earlier, her heart started to thump anyway. Silently her door swung open and two dark figures entered her room.

"Papa?" she called softly.

"Yes, Korinna, it's me. This is Herr Krugmann," her father said.

Korinna could see the second man nod to her through the darkness. *"Guten Abend,"* she said.

Her father pulled the wardrobe away from the wall. "Sophie," he called into the dark hole. "Sophie, wake up."

"Bernd? What is it? What's happened? Are the Gestapo here?" Her voice, even in a whisper, sounded shrill and full of fear.

"No, Sophie. Don't worry. I have a surprise for you. Look who's here."

"Who? I can't see. Who is it?" Her voice still sounded nervous.

"Papa?" queried a small voice. "Papa!" Rachel exclaimed.

"Shhhhh," Korinna's father warned.

"Sol?" Sophie said, sounding incredulous. "Rachel get back here," she said to her daughter, who had jumped out of the hole and was standing in Korinna's room.

"It's alright," Herr Rehme said. "She can come out. You can come out, too. Just be quiet."

Herr Krugmann picked up his daughter and hugged her tight. "My little Rachel, my little Rachel," he said, emotion strangling his voice and making it sound gruff. Gently he set her back on the floor. By this time Frau Krugmann also stood in Korinna's room, staring up at her husband. Herr Krugmann pulled his wife into his arms. "Oh, Sophie, how I have missed you."

Korinna looked down at her tightly clasped hands, embarrassed to be witnessing such a scene. She felt like an intruder in her own bedroom. But she couldn't very well slip out of her small room unnoticed with all these people filling it.

She peeked up to see Herr Krugmann pick up Rachel again. The three of them huddled together with their arms around each other.

"Now you must all hide again," Herr Rehme said. "It will be even more cramped for you, but we'll try to move you on as soon as possible. Your next stop has

opened up and is waiting for you. Now it's just a matter of getting you there safely."

Herr Krugmann gripped Korinna's father's hand as Rachel and Frau Krugmann crawled through the wall, out of view. "Thank you for everything," he said, his voice catching in his throat. "I am so thankful for you."

"We do what we can and wish it were more," Korinna's father said.

They stood a moment in silence, each one thinking his own thoughts, then Herr Krugmann crouched and crawled behind the wall.

Korinna's father closed the wardrobe and turned to his daughter. "Go to sleep now." He hugged Korinna, and she wanted to cling to him when he released her, but she didn't. She withdrew into her pillows and watched the dark image of her father leave her room.

She closed her eyes and heard the soft rustling and whispering coming from behind her wardrobe. She realized her father hadn't closed the wardrobe completely against the wall. She waited for the noises to quiet down, but soon realized they wouldn't. The Krugmanns hadn't seen each other for weeks, and for who knows how long before they had come here.

Korinna slipped out of bed and quietly tiptoed out of her room. She stood in the doorway of her parents' bedroom and listened to their even breathing. The floor was cold on her feet. Silently she crawled onto her parents' bed and nestled in the warm and secure valley between her mother and father. And there she finally fell asleep.

———————

The next morning Korinna walked to school alone. Rita hadn't waited for her as she usually did, which was fine with Korinna. She wasn't in the mood for Rita anyway.

She got to school just before the first lesson started, so she slipped into her chair and looked over to Eva. Usually Eva would look back at her and they would smile good morning to each other if they hadn't walked to school together. But this morning Eva didn't even glance in her direction. Korinna shrugged and turned her attention to the teacher.

When school was out at one, she found Eva and Rita and a few other girls huddled outside the big doors. They were all going straight to the meeting instead of home for dinner because they had much to prepare for the Führer's visit. The group broke up as Korinna advanced.

"Hello," Korinna said.

"*Heil Hitler,*" Rita said.

Eva avoided her glance and kept her eyes on the cement sidewalk.

"Are you going to the *Jungmädel* meeting?" Rita asked.

"I'm wearing my uniform, aren't I?"

"I was just asking," Rita said. "I thought you'd be too tired or too sick or something."

Korinna looked at Eva, but Eva was still examining the sidewalk. She held her growing anger in check. "I'm fine. I have been for days now."

"You've been acting strange, if you ask me," Rita said.

Korinna felt the blood drain out of her face. Why was Rita acting this way? Why wouldn't Eva look at her? What was going on?

"And you look terrible," Rita continued. "You have big bags under your eyes. Don't you sleep at night? Or is something keeping you awake?"

"Let's go to the meeting," Eva said, interrupting. "We don't want to be late." She started walking away from the two best friends.

Korinna turned from Rita and followed Eva.

Rita quickly caught up and passed Korinna so that she could walk beside Eva. Korinna stared at their backs.

A warm front had moved into the area the night before, and the piles of snow were turning to slush. People walked with their coats unbuttoned and a spring in their steps. Korinna watched Rita's and Eva's opened coats whip behind them in the wind as they walked. She walked stiffly, well aware of the surreptitious glances she was getting from the other girls on their way to the meeting.

A memory came back to Korinna as she walked. She felt as if she were no longer in her body, but watching this scene from a different angle. That's because she *had* viewed this scene from a different angle before, she realized. She remembered the day Anita Scheinmann had been ostracized from her friends for being a Jew. Korinna now remembered that she had been one of the ringleaders to plan Anita's humiliation. And that's how she knew, so positively, that the same thing was now happening to her.

The *Jungmädel* meeting passed much the same way

the walk from school had passed. No one talked directly to her, but everyone watched her.

More than once she almost ran out of the room. But pressing her lips together to keep them from trembling, she had lifted her chin and stayed. Whatever was going on, she reassured herself, would be cleared up, and things would go back to the way they were.

"Rita," Korinna said, when she found her friend alone in the back of the room. "What's going on? Why are you ignoring me?"

Rita looked around. "Nothing's going on."

Korinna placed a hand on her best friend's arm. "What do you mean, *nothing?* No one will speak to me, even you, my best friend." She hated the quaver she heard in her voice.

"I'm not ignoring you, I'm just busy," Rita said resentfully. "We have a lot to do before the parade, and if you don't care, I do!"

"Of course I . . . I . . ."

"See? You can't even say it, Korinna Rehme. You don't even care that our beloved Führer is coming to this city!"

"But I do!"

"You don't show it," Rita said, practically spitting out the words, and she walked away.

When the meeting ended, Korinna didn't bother waiting to be humiliated further, she simply put on her coat and left.

Outside, the air was cooling down, but Korinna

didn't button up her coat. She didn't care if she caught pneumonia. She just didn't care. Maybe she'd be better off like Ruth, she thought bitterly. Then all those awful girls, especially Rita, would be sorry for how they'd treated her!

That was a stupid, childish way to think, thought Korinna quickly, and immediately she regretted it. She knew Ruth would rather be alive today, even if it meant hiding in a hole.

"Korinna, don't stop and don't turn around."

Korinna recognized the voice. It was Eva. She started to turn around.

"I said *don't* turn around! Keep walking!" Eva's voice sounded hoarse. But then Korinna realized it was because she was trying to whisper loud enough to be heard by Korinna, but not by anyone else.

"What are you doing? What's going on?" Korinna, too, kept her voice down.

"I don't have time to explain," Eva whispered. "But I have to warn you. Your house is going to be searched tonight."

Korinna felt weak with fear. She hadn't wanted to think that it could happen again. But she'd known there must have been some terrible reason for the way she'd been treated today. Now she knew. Somehow the Gestapo had found out about the Krugmanns.

"How do you know?"

"Just believe me," Eva said urgently.

"Why are you telling me this?"

"Because you're my friend, Korinna. Bye."

"Eva, wait!" Korinna said frantically. She wanted to know more, but there was no reply. She turned around. Eva was gone.

Korinna broke into a run, but just as quickly she stopped. If anyone saw her running home it would look suspicious. If her house were going to be searched tonight, that meant that the Gestapo weren't *sure* the Rehmes were doing something wrong. If they knew about the Krugmanns definitely, Korinna didn't think they'd wait until dark to search the house. They'd do it immediately to keep the Jews from escaping.

She didn't run, but she walked quickly. She saw no one except for a few soldiers, but they were so common it was as if they weren't even there. And she also saw a small family of three, riding past her on their bikes. They all ignored her except the little girl, sitting behind the father, who stared and waved. Korinna absently waved back.

Finally she was home. She burst through the front door calling, "Mother! Mother, are you home?"

"Korinna!" Her mother came running to her from the kitchen. "How are you? I've been worried sick about you. I would have come out to get you, but Papa wouldn't let me. He said—"

"Calm down, Helga," Korinna's father said, interrupting his wife as he joined them in the front hall. He took his distraught wife into his arms and hugged her. "Korinna's home now, everything is going to be fine."

Frau Rehme took a deep breath. "I'm better now. I was just so worried. But now we're all home safe."

"Then you know?" Korinna said, looking at her parents.

"Know what?" her father asked.

"About the search. We're going to be searched tonight. Eva told me."

"Are you sure?" her mother said sharply.

Korinna nodded. "I have to go warn the Krugmanns. We have to hide them, Papa! What if the Gestapo finds them?"

"It's okay, Korinna—" began her father, but Korinna interrupted him.

"I have to tell them!" she cried, moving toward the stairs. She knew she sounded panicky, but she couldn't control herself. She had to tell them now, before it was too late!

"Korinna, stop!" her father commanded firmly, holding her gently in his arms. "They're gone," he said, staring down into his daughter's eyes.

"Gone?" she repeated.

"You may have even passed them on the street," her mother said softly.

Tears welled up in Korinna's eyes. "You mean the Gestapo already found them? Are they going to shoot the Krugmanns? Are we going to go to jail?"

"No, no," said her father gently, still holding her. "No police have been here yet. The Krugmanns have escaped. They're on their way to their next hiding place."

Korinna was confused. "But you said I may have passed them on the street. How could that be? It's still a little light out."

"Let's go sit down and I'll make tea," Korinna's mother said, leading them into the kitchen.

While her mother heated the water, her father explained what had happened.

"When I got to school this morning, I was let go. I was told I was no longer wanted as a teacher, so I came home. I knew immediately it was because I was under suspicion for something, and that I was probably being watched.

"On my way home, I stopped by the tailor's to pick up a shirt he was mending, and then I came home. You see, the tailor is a friend, and he sent a message. This afternoon, three people came to visit. They came noisily and happily because we hadn't seen each other for such a long time. They stayed for an hour, and then they left as they came, out the front door."

"But what does this have to do with the Krugmanns?" Korinna asked, trying to hold back her tears.

"The three who came to visit were of the approximate age and size of the Krugmanns. When they were here they traded clothes with the Krugmanns, and it was the Krugmanns who left by the front door and pedaled away on their bicycles, not the others."

Stunned, Korinna realized it could have been Rachel waving to her from the back of the bicycle as her father pedaled past.

"So those others are still here. Are they hiding upstairs?" she finally asked.

"They went out the back way," Frau Rehme said, bringing over hot cups of weak tea to the table where Korinna and her father were sitting.

"If anyone was watching the front, the same people who came in left. Nothing suspicious there. And if anyone was watching the back alley, three people left, all of them staunch supporters of Hitler. Even if they are stopped and questioned, they will be safe."

No longer could she hold back her tears.

"Korinna, everything has worked out. Everyone is safe," her mother said, trying to console her daughter. "There's no reason for tears."

"But they must think I hate them," Korinna cried.

"I'm sure they don't think that," her father soothed, stroking her back.

"They saw how you cared for Rachel, Korinna. They knew how you felt," her mother said.

"But I never even hugged her. I—I never told her I cared."

"She knew, *Liebling*, she knew."

The family sat silent for a few minutes.

"I fear it is not safe for us here," her father said quietly.

Korinna's heart thudded painfully. "But the Krugmanns are gone."

Herr Rehme shook his head. "If the Gestapo finds the hidden room, they'll know what we did to help Jews, even though the Krugmanns are safely away."

"What will we do?"

Her mother covered her hand with one of hers. "We will have to leave as soon as possible." She glanced at her husband. "Tonight?"

He nodded slowly. "As soon as it is dark . . . if the Gestapo doesn't come first." He turned to his daughter. "Go upstairs and rest now, *Liebling.*"

Korinna rose on trembling legs. It was hard to believe that little Rachel wasn't waiting for her behind her bedroom wall. And that Sophie, with her suspicious eyes, and Herr Krugmann weren't there, . . . and that Ruth was gone.

Her room didn't look any different, but it felt empty, silent, lonely.

She would never forget them, she vowed fiercely as she retrieved Rachel's drawings from under her mattress. She would not forget what they looked like, the way Rachel had forgotten what her sister looked like. She would never forget. Roughly, she wiped the tears from her eyes. If the Gestapo were coming tonight, perhaps any minute, she had a lot of work to do. She could rest later.

Holding the packet of Rachel's drawings, she looked around the room for a suitable hiding place. She didn't want anyone to find them.

After she'd hidden the drawings, she picked up the packet of *Jungmädel* pamphlets she had received last week. She opened one and looked through it. She felt as if she had aged years since she had first held these pamphlets in her hands. Then the shiny paper and the photograph of Adolf Hitler on the front had so impressed her. Now they just made her palms sweat. But they would do, she thought, standing up. For what she wanted, they would do perfectly.

Chapter Fourteen

As soon as the sky turned dark, the Gestapo came. This time they didn't bother knocking on the door, they just broke the lock and stomped right in.

Korinna tried to swallow past the lump of fear that closed her throat, but it was impossible. She saw that one of the officers was Hans Damerau. Oh, how she despised him for hitting her father. She couldn't believe she had ever looked up to him.

This time there were four men. They started in the front room and destroyed it. They knocked holes in the walls, and ripped open the sofas, and pulled up floor boards. The only thing they didn't touch was the framed picture of Adolf Hitler, hanging above the ruined couch.

Turning on every light, they worked their way through the kitchen. Again, they destroyed everything. Korinna's father had warned her and her mother not to say anything when the Gestapo was here, no matter what they did. And Korinna could see her mother biting her lip until she drew blood. Korinna could taste the metallic tang of fear in her own mouth.

The Rehmes followed the officers upstairs. There was barely enough room for the three of them with the four men tossing things about. They started in Korinna's parents' bedroom. First the bed was ripped open, and the feathers danced merrily around the room, oblivious to the seriousness of the situation. Then their wardrobe was dismantled with an ax, as were the chair and Herr Rehme's desk, which had been in the family for three generations. It was priceless. Now it was worthless.

Korinna watched everything as if she were watching a play. She felt involved, yet somehow removed. She felt angry, yet on the verge of hysterical laughter. This was not happening to her or to her family. How could it be? They were good, loyal Germans. They loved their Fatherland, didn't they? They wanted Germany to prosper and succeed, didn't they? What more was needed? Only that they had to hate Jews, love their Führer, and obey the party at all costs. Not too much. Maybe she could convince her parents before it was too late, she thought frantically. She could convince Hans it had all been a mistake. Her parents weren't traitors, they were just ignorant. They didn't know better. She knew she could explain everything. Hans would understand. After all, he was her best friend's brother.

"Hans!" she cried.

"Korinna, silence!" her father commanded.

Her mother put a firm arm around her and said quietly, "Hush, *Liebling*. It'll be over soon. Hush."

Korinna could feel her mother's arm shake, and it flowed through her own body until she could feel her legs quiver with fear. What had she almost done? She had almost ruined everything! She had almost turned in her parents!

Her legs trembled uncontrollably. Two officers were now in the bathroom. She heard a grating noise, and then the sound of flowing water. As her mother led her into her bedroom behind Hans and one of the other officers, she saw a flood of water flowing out of the bathroom. Their house would be ruined.

Her bedroom received the same treatment as her parents' room had. Only the picture of the Führer above her desk remained untouched.

They destroyed the wardrobe, but still the back of it stayed in place over the damning hole in the wall. Hans lifted the ax one last time.

"Stop!" Herr Rehme said.

Hans turned to look at Korinna's father. "I thought you learned your lesson last time," he said viciously. "But I guess I was wrong," he added as he nodded to one of the other officers.

The other officer grabbed Herr Rehme from behind and pinned his arms behind his back. The third officer punched Korinna's father in the stomach, just below the ribs, leaving him gasping for breath.

"Stop it!" Korinna cried. "Leave him alone!"

"Get back there," Hans said, easily pushing Korinna back into the corner of the room. "Don't interfere," he said menacingly. Again he lifted the ax and it came down hard, splintering the back of the wardrobe. The ax came down again and the back of the wardrobe fell away in two parts, exposing the hole in the wall.

"Lights, quickly," Hans demanded, obviously in charge of this search.

Another officer stepped forward with two flashlights, which they swung around the hidden room.

Korinna looked over at her father. He sat on the floor, breathing normally now. Her mother squatted next to him. Both of their faces were white and pinched with fear. Korinna knew they expected to be arrested at any moment.

She looked back at Hans, who was now partially in the hidden room. All she could see of him were his shiny leather boots and the gleaming pistol attached around his waist. She swallowed nervously. If her plan didn't work, she wondered if they would be shot on the spot.

Hans poked his head back out. "What is this room?" he demanded.

"It's no use," said Korinna's father, sighing wearily. He started to say more, but his daughter interrupted him.

"It's my room," Korinna said, sounding more brazen than she felt. All the eyes turn to her. "I use it as kind of a—secret clubhouse."

"Korinna, what are you talking about?" her mother cried shrilly.

She turned to her mother. "I never told you two about it because I thought you might not like how involved I am in the *Jungmädel*. You always say I have to spend more time on my homework," she said, hoping she sounded disdainful. She turned back to Hans. "I keep all my party material back there. And when my parents think I'm studying, I go back there."

Hans's eyes narrowed. "How did you bolt the wardrobe to the wall?"

Korinna tried to shrug with what she hoped looked like nonchalance. "I just did. I used screws and hinges. I did it one day when no one was home."

Hans narrowed his eyes. "It's not easy to drill holes in the wall."

"I'm strong," Korinna countered. "Didn't Rita tell you that I'm the strongest girl in our *Jungmädel?* I can run the fastest, too."

"Strong enough to move the wardrobe?"

Korinna waved her hand, hoping Hans wouldn't notice that it trembled slightly. "I first took out all the drawers and my clothes. It wasn't so heavy after that."

Hans glared at her before looking in the small room again. Korinna knew he saw all the pamphlets she had spread around the space, and the clippings she had saved of the Führer she had pinned to the walls. She had even piled the Krugmann's blankets and mattresses on top of each other and covered them with a small woven rug to make the room more appealing. She wanted to convince anyone who found it, that it was a comfortable place to be. Only a very loyal German would create such a shrine to the National Socialist Party.

"This is a trick!"

Korinna's heart jumped into her mouth. Why didn't Hans believe her?

"Korinna, how could you?" demanded her mother, wiping her eyes. "We always thought you were studying. We didn't want to keep you from your interest in the party, we too love the party, but how will you pass your classes if you don't study?"

"I did study," she said, trying to sound sullen. "I just wanted a place to pin all my clippings. You said it would ruin the walls if I pinned them out here."

"Korinna," her father said sternly. "You've disobeyed us and you will have to be punished."

"But I—"

"Enough!" Hans shouted. He stood up, looking uncertainly at Korinna for a brief moment, then he quickly put on a fierce scowl. "I have information."

Korinna didn't like the triumphant sound she heard in his voice. She watched as he extracted a black book from his jacket pocket. *Her black book.* Only one person could have gotten that book and given it to Hans—her best friend.

She felt dizzy staring up at Hans. Now she would surely be shot as a traitor. No more would she walk through the beautiful countryside. No more would she smell the sweet flowers of spring. No more would she feel the bite of the cold winter wind. No more would she hug her mother and—

"Answer me!"

Korinna looked up at Hans through a rosy haze. Maybe she was dying already.

"Why did you tear out a page in this book?" Hans demanded.

Then she remembered. She *had* torn out the page. Those awful five words—*My parents are the enemy*. Rita had read those words, but she had no proof.

"I—I made a drawing I didn't like and I ripped the page out. I threw it away."

Hans sneered at her. "You lie! You wrote that your parents were traitors, Jew-lovers, scum. Why didn't you turn them in?"

"That's not true!" Korinna cried. "It was a drawing, a drawing of my cat!"

Hans stared furiously down at Korinna, and then his eyes shifted to her parents. "I don't believe this!" he stormed. "I don't believe any of this!" He stomped his boot on the wooden floor in his anger. "I will find the truth, and then you will be sent to prison! I'll make sure you never get out!" He turned to his fellow officers. "Come!" he commanded, his voice taut with anger and suppressed violence.

Just at that moment, *Tag* pranced into the room, and one of the officers nearly tripped over her. Hans glared at the tiny kitten. Before Korinna realized what was about to happen, he aimed his shiny boot at the animal and viciously kicked out at *Tag*. The kitten jumped aside at the last second.

Korinna cried out. Images of Herr Haase came suddenly into her mind. She had stood and watched him get kicked and beaten, but this time she would stop the brutality. She tried to move, but it was too late. Hans kicked at the kitten a second time. This time his boot connected, leaving the animal lying on her side, unmoving.

Hans waved the other officers out, and they preceded him through the bedroom door. Hans stopped and turned in the doorway to glare back at the Rehmes. "I smell Jews," he said viciously. "I smell their dirty, rotten stink. And when I find them, they'll lead me right back to you!"

Chapter Fifteen

Korinna pressed her hand against her mouth. She wouldn't give those pigs the satisfaction of hearing her cry. As she listened to the car roar down the street, an uncontrollable trembling settled deep within her. It sent shock waves out to the furthest extremities of her body, so that her hands shook and her legs quivered. Even her lips trembled against her hand.

"It's all right," she heard her father say to her mother in a comforting voice. "Hush, my love, hush."

Korinna felt her own tears start to flow. She crawled through the feathers and splinters, which now littered the floor. Gently, she picked up *Tag*. The kitten quivered and then seemed to shake herself awake. Korinna smiled through her tears and kissed *Tag* on the nose. Her parents wrapped their arms around her, and they all gave in to their tears. Even her father cried, something she had never seen him do before.

Nothing mattered anymore. There was nothing left

to care about, or so it seemed, Korinna thought as she looked around her destroyed room. But of course there was a lot to care about, she corrected herself. She cared about her parents, and the Krugmanns, whom she'd never see again, and about her Fatherland. There was a lot of caring left to do, she realized with relief.

Her tears were fewer now, and they dried on her cheeks, making her skin feel stiff and uncomfortable. She looked up to see her father's tears had been wiped away, as if they had never been. Just like the Krugmanns, she thought. Like all enemies to the Fatherland. They were being wiped away so that someday it would seem as if they had never existed.

"We have to leave now," her father said quietly.

"Where are we going?" Korinna asked.

"It's best if you don't know until we get there, *Liebling,*" her father said gently.

Korinna stroked *Tag's* silken head. "We're leaving forever?"

"Maybe we can come back someday," her mother said.

"But right now it's too dangerous to stay," her father said.

"What about my school?" Korinna asked. "What about my friends?" Then she remembered she didn't have any friends anymore. Only Eva had been brave enough to be her friend at the end when she'd really needed one.

"There will be other schools and other friends," Korinna's mother said reassuringly.

Her father rose to his feet and helped his wife up. "We have to hurry and pack. Take only what you absolutely need. We'll be traveling a great distance tonight."

Korinna stood up beside her parents. "How will we get there?"

"I've hidden bicycles out back, for just such an emergency."

"But won't they be watching us?"

"They won't expect us to leave tonight. Hans will think we feel too scared to dare escape. Or maybe he thinks we are stupid enough to feel too safe."

Korinna reached out for her mother's hand. "I'm frightened."

"That's okay," her mother said. She drew Korinna close to her and hugged her tightly. "We're all frightened. But that's natural. It's when we feel at ease and certain of ourselves that we make mistakes."

Korinna thought about how she had felt so confident yesterday that Rita was a true friend. Rita felt sorry for the Jews, and Korinna had been glad to hear it. She had actually believed it! Instead, if she had been frightened and wary, she never would have said so much to Rita about her feelings for the Jews. She was certain that was what had instigated this search. That and her black book.

"Hurry," her father said. "The sooner we leave, the

better. Put everything in your book bag," he added, pointing to the leather bag half buried in the debris. He looked at the kitten in her arms. "Where we are going, you can't take a pet. We'll have to leave *Tag* with friends along the way."

Korinna could only nod mutely in reply.

Her mother gave her one last squeeze and then followed Herr Rehme out of the room. Korinna went to the hanging picture of the Führer and took it off the wall. Tied to the back of it were Rachel's drawings. She put them in the bag. She looked around her room. What else did she need? She gathered some undergarments, a sweater, a wool skirt, and an extra scarf. All of this fit into her book bag with hardly any room to spare. She found a few sheets of paper and a pencil in the mess on the floor, and stuffed those on top of everything and closed the leather bag.

Taking the bag with her and tucking *Tag* under her arm, Korinna walked to her door and shut off the light. Looking back, she could barely see in the darkness that immediately took over her room. But that was better. In the dark she could imagine her room as it had been before — before all this. But no, she didn't want to remember it before the Krugmanns, as if they had never been here.

She looked to where her wardrobe had stood. The hole in the wall was darker even than the room. It looked like a gaping wound.

Now she had to leave. She didn't know where she was going, but she had a feeling it was going to be her turn to hide behind someone else's bedroom wall, in a dark, small hole with barely enough air to breathe. And if she never came back to this house, it would be because ... because. ... She couldn't bring herself to finish that thought.

She just hoped she would meet the Krugmanns again someday—someday in the future when all people were free to speak and act without fear.

Suddenly, it dawned on her what could possibly be just as important as love, if not more so.

Freedom.

She ran to tell her parents.

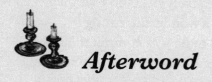

Afterword

The story you have just read is about a fictional character named Korinna Rehme. Korinna, like eight million real children, belonged to one of Hitler's youth groups that existed before and during World War II.

Why did children get so involved in their youth groups, even to the point of reporting "un-German" teachers, friends, and parents? Research and interviews have since shown that these girls and boys were brainwashed into believing what they did was for a good cause.

In 1933, Germany was in a depression. Poor and out of work, many people looked for someone to lead them to a brighter future. Hitler promised to do this.

Hitler said he would create a strong country and a Thousand-Year Reich, yet no one knew how he would do this. But because everyone wanted it so desperately, they followed him blindly.

Children, especially, were affected. And why not?

They had a lot of fun at their Hitler youth group meetings. They sang, hiked, helped the elderly, raised money, and baked. They marched in parades and practiced sports. And because Hitler controlled all the radio broadcasts, all the newspapers and books that were printed, the children truly believed that they were helping him create a wonderful, strong Fatherland. All they had to do was commit their lives to the cause, report anyone who seemed un-German, and hate the enemies.

But who were the enemies? Anyone who looked different. Anyone who acted different. The followers of Hitler specifically targeted Jews (and anyone who helped them), Eastern Europeans, mentally and physically challenged people, gypsies, and homosexuals, to name a few.

Hitler's followers murdered over six million Jews and millions of other people, too, before and during World War II. It is estimated that, by the end of the war, over two-thirds of the Jews in Europe had been murdered. Well over one million of them were children like Rachel.

Even knowing they could be killed for helping "the enemy," some Gentiles (non-Jewish people like the Rehmes), especially outside Germany, put their lives in danger to help the victims. Ten thousand Rachels may have survived because of these decent human beings. Because no records were kept of hidden children, it is impossible to know if this number is accurate or if as many as several hundred thousand children survived.

I ended this novel with Korinna's realization that freedom is perhaps more important than love. After all, if you're not free to love whom you wish, what good is love?

Laura E. Williams was born in Seoul, Korea. She has lived in Belgium, Hawaii, and, for a few months, on a sailboat on the Caribbean. In 1983 Laura graduated from Denison University with a double major in English and art, and in 1988 she graduated from Trinity College with an M.A. in literary writing. She also earned a masters in education from St. Joseph College. She currently lives in Connecticut, where she is a teacher of high-school English.